Books by William Keisling

Three Mile Island: Turning Point
Solar Water Heating Systems
The Sins of Our Fathers
The Meltdown

WILLIAM KEISLING
THE MELTDOWN
or, the bologna merchants

YARDBIRD
Philadelphia & Bar Harbor

Copyright © 1990 by William Keisling
All rights reserved.
ISBN 0-9620251-2-7 (Hardcover)
ISBN 0-9620251-3-5 (Softcover)
FIRST EDITION

Excerpts from this book previously appeared in
The Crescent Review and *Rolling Stone Magazine.*
The author gratefully acknowledges that the writing of this book was supported jointly by a grant from the Pennsylvania Council on the Arts and the National Endowment for the Arts, a federal agency.

Cover painting by Lynn Hamrick
The lyrics appearing on page 92 are from Caravan, by Van Morrison, © 1969 Warner Brothers Music Corp., Caledonia Soul Music. All rights administered by Warner Brothers Music Corporation. Used by permission of Warner/Chappell Music, Inc. All rights reserved.

This book is printed on acid-free paper. Set in Garamond. Typeset and manufactured in the United States of America.

Yardbird Books
Orders Department
P.O. Box 10214
State College, Pennsylvania 16805

Library of Congress Cataloging-in-Publication Data

Keisling, William
    The meltdown, or, The bologna merchants / William Keisling.
      p. cm.
    ISBN 0-9620251-2-7 (alk. paper) -- ISBN 0-9620251-3-5 (pbk. : alk. paper)
      1. Three Mile Island Nuclear Power Plant (Pa.)--Fiction.
I. Title. II. Title: Meltdown. III. Title: Bologna Merchants.
PS3561.E37575M45 1990
813'.54--dc20   89-24833
                                            CIP

This book is for Lauren, Eowyn & Ariel

"Things just very rarely go haywire anymore."
	Andre Gregor *in conversation*

"When I make a mistake it's a beaut."
	Fiorello La Guardia

"It's the nearest thing to a meltdown that I ever want to see."
	John Phelan
	Chairman, New York Stock Exchange

THE MELTDOWN

1.

When I was a boy in grade school I knew a girl named Sally Nex. All the mothers used to say she was a bad girl. Older boys used to go around the neighborhood painting the words "Nex is Sex" all over everything. You'd always see Sally's father, poor old Mr. Nex, tirelessly whitewashing telephone poles and bridge abutments to hide the offending words. When she was only in the sixth grade the police found Sally in an abandoned house with five high school boys and a hash pipe. In those days I didn't know what a hash pipe was, didn't even know what sex was, though I knew both had something to do with mysterious Mona Lisa-smiling Sally Nex.

I ran into Sally Nex years later, when I was a young man of twenty. I would not have run into her again had I not decided to stick around town. At the time I worked for a small magazine. In those days I'd walk the streets of town, a pen in each pocket, like six-shooters, caring only about my God-almighty career. Nothing more. Then one morning I answered the phone to hear an anonymous, gay-sounding man say he was in love. He was calling everyone in the book to let the world know.

"Big deal," I told him.

"And you," he asked me, "what about you, young man? Are you in love?"

"I don't have time."

"Well you're missing out on something."

Not long after that Sally Nex came back into my life. By now she was a lusty, curvacious young woman in her mid-twenties. At loose ends, she'd done the West Coast thing for a few years before hitting bottom and coming home. One of the women on our editorial board invited Sally to volunteer at the magazine.

The day Sally Nex came to the office two men from the editorial board and a college intern followed her around. All three had tongues hanging from their mouths. They tripped over each other to follow Sally Nex around the office. She went about her chores, asking "Has anybody seen the waxer?" and they'd all scramble for it. I watched the spectacle from the sidelines with one of the magazine's writers, Jack Falstaff.

"Why do I get the impression they're following her around like she's a bitch in heat?" Falstaff wondered aloud. A parade of tongue-outhanging men trailed Sally up and down the steps. "Of course, not that promiscuity isn't normal for someone her age. At ah, twenty-five, twenty-six that's, ah, normal behavior," he said, flicking the ash off his hand-rolled cigarette, his eyes roving around like they always did.

Not long afterward Sally seduced our intern. She did it for a lark, breaking his heart when he learned it was only a fling. Men on the editorial board often seduced the female interns, treating each seduction like a notch on a belt. Eyebrows were raised when Sally Nex turned the tables and seduced her intern.

I felt sorry for Pete, the intern, even though he was an incredibly lousy reporter. Once I assigned him to look into a fire at the high school. The school principal had taken to fighting vandalism by locking the fire extinguishers behind iron bars.

When the building caught fire one day no one could get to the fire extinguishers. Pete came back from his interview with the principal and said there was no problem. I asked if he was an idiot. He said he didn't want to anger anyone.

"Why go stirring things up?" he wanted to know.

"It's our job to stir things up!"

Anyway, lousy reporter or not, I felt sorry for him. One night after Sally Nex ditched him I took him down to the hotel to listen to jazz.

"I can't believe it," Pete finally said after a few beers. He'd loosened up and was rubbing his hair with his hand. "She said there was nothing to it. 'Nothing to it at all,' she says. She just wanted a little nooky. 'Can't you understand that?'"

"Oh, that's tough."

"'Nothing to it at all,' she says."

"Have another beer, Pete. Why don't you forget about it."

"How can I forget about it?"

"You can try. Have another beer."

I paid the waitress for another round.

Pete just couldn't get over it.

"'It's nothing but sex,' she says. Can you believe it? What a whore. 'Oh I get it,' I told her. 'You've just got back from the West Coast. That's how they are on the West Coast, isn't it?' That must be what the West Coast does to a woman."

"Listen here Pete. Sally's just casual about it. That's all."

"Yeah well she's a whore."

"Listen. If it makes you feel any better Sally's always been like that. Ever since she was young. Did I ever tell you I went to grade school with her? Between you and me, can I tell you something?"

"Sure."

"Between you and me?"

"Sure."

"I wouldn't want this to get around, but when Sally Nex was

a girl in grade school boys used to go around painting the words 'Nex is Sex' all over the neighborhood. You'd always see her old man out whitewashing over the words."

I was a little tipsy. I wondered if I should have said anything. Pete sat staring at me with widening eyes. The bass player bowed his bass. I tried to listen.

"Do you think she's a nympho?"

"I don't know what that means. You never hear a man called that."

Pete seemed to have talked it all out. He let it drop. He sat looking into his beer, thinking.

The next morning I came to work early and found Sally Nex in the front office, using the phones. She wore a loose cotton dress. On such a warm, late summer day the dress wonderfully suited her. After all those years I was alone with Sally Nex.

I tried striking up a conversation, stuttering out that I'd always associated her with sex, ever since I was a boy. It didn't sound right coming out. I had trouble finding words. My heart was an unknown galaxy to me. I told Sally I remembered how her old man used to run around the neighborhood whitewashing the words "Nex is Sex" from bridge abutments and phone poles. She smiled in a hurt way.

She said a bad reputation had always followed her, for no other reason she could think of than her last name rhymed with sex. Men got the wrong idea about her, she said. That's why she'd left the West Coast, hoping to escape back into the simpler small-town life. But now things were starting up again. She said she was moved to get counseling. In fact, she said, she'd been on the phone trying to line up a shrink when I came in. I felt sorry for her. I touched her shoulder, left her alone with the phone.

Later that morning I went into the bathroom and found the words "Nex is Sex" scrawled in pencil among the graffiti on the wall. The words took their place among such chestnuts as "God is dead — Nietzsche," "Nietzsche is dead, things are back to normal — God," and "Illiterate? Write for free pamphlet."

A few days after that I was in a car with some friends when we passed the big welcome sign at the edge of town. Someone had painted "Nex is Sex" at the bottom of the sign, in big ugly black letters. In the next few days I'd see those words in what seemed like a hundred places, scrawled in quick black letters all over town.

The next week I came early into the office and encountered, in the bathroom, an old, graying man. A can of paint in hand, he was whitewashing over the words "Nex is Sex."

2.

Jack Falstaff was a big talker. By that I don't mean to say he liked to talk, though he certainly did like to do that. He was a big man. Six foot three or four inches tall. He weighed at least three hundred and twenty-five pounds. Falstaff was one of those big men who dominated a room when he came in. He'd been an all-star linebacker in school, at Duke University. Don't think though that I was impressed. He used to bore me to death with his old football stories.

His family hailed from New York. Someplace on Long Island. A bedrock family, with holdings in things and a summer home far out on the island. Falstaff broke the family mold. After he'd left Duke and the football he'd spent many years tending bar in DC. He'd come to town in the early seventies, worked at some sort of pottery and crafts collective. Turning pots and urns. Making candles. I still can't picture it. Soon thereafter he fell in with the bunch at the magazine. Down on his luck, he took a cramped room on the second floor of the magazine office.

That the magazine should shelter Jack Falstaff in his time of need seemed altogether appropriate. The magazine was after all our town's safety-deposit box for bankrupt liberalism. It lingered on with the last of the great alternative rags, founded in the selfless, turbulent days of the Vietnam War, struggling for direction and purpose after the draft had ended. People idealistically worked there a few years, burned out, then left to join the real world.

The magazine had its offices in a rundown row house in the poor part of town. The building housed a motley collection of tiny liberal organizations: a bail program, a fair-housing council, an anti-nuclear group. A wrinkled, faded drawing of H.L. Mencken graced one of the magazine's shabby walls.

The first time I saw Jack Falstaff I thought he was the most important man I'd ever seen. By then he was a writer-in-residence at the magazine, living in the cramped room on the second floor. I'd never seen a writer before. I guess I mistook him for Horace Greeley, or maybe the creased picture of Mencken on the wall. This was back in the days when I first started writing for the magazine. Falstaff by this time had begun keeping two mangy dogs in his room. I'd come sheepishly up the steps to the office, seeking my first writing assignment, when a massive, portly man opened the door to what appeared to be a junked-up bedroom. He came out into the hallway, the dogs at his heels.

I got the assignment, but was shocked to discover the magazine paid little or no salaries. For a while the rag didn't even have an editor. Every Wednesday the editorial board met in the shabby front office where we'd collectively copy edit each issue. An article would be passed from one editorial board member to the next. One person would correct the article to suit his or her fancy, then pass it on to the next board member, who might cross out the previous corrections, making new ones. By the time it had been corrected by all dozen or so board members the article would be unintelligible.

One board member, a retired high school teacher named

Irving Brodsky, never failed each week to stand and lecture us on Marx and Engels. We might be discussing mundane matters like how we were going to pay the month's light bill when up he would come to jabber away on Marx's views on the exploitation of the proletariat.

The editorial board never was much too concerned about the business side of publishing. The board once chased away our only good ad salesman because he'd committed the capital offense of calling one of the college interns a girl.

"Just give it to one of the girls to type," the salesman said one day when he came into the office with ad copy.

You'd have thought he'd kidnapped Lindbergh's baby. His offhand remark sparked what came to be known as the Great Feminist Inquisition. The women on the board went on the warpath, forcing through a written policy directive demanding that henceforth all female humans had to be addressed as "women," regardless of age. This included eight-year-old women. The ad salesmen called it bullshit and left. Who'd blame him?

Shortly thereafter another board member rose to suggest we capitalize the "b" in black to atone for hundreds of years of forced servitude of the Negro race. Irving Brodsky, the retired high school teacher, pulled out a handkerchief and sobbed outright. He never failed to choke up whenever we discussed civil rights. "I think this is the very least we can do for The Black Man," he choked out. Despite his emotional plea this motion fell through because no one wanted to also capitalize the "w" in white. One board member reasoned white people already had enough going for them.

This unique editorial system obviously wasn't working. I lobbied hard for the return of a single editor, thinking sooner or later I'd get the job.

Over the years we'd had a succession of editors, who'd all made the fatal mistake of sleeping with one of the board members, Nancy Downs. It hadn't escaped my notice that Nancy Downs had a habit of seducing whomever happened to be editor. It also didn't escape my notice that shortly after the seduction the editor would always go crazy and resign. It happened five or six times.

Not that she limited her conquests to editors. During the Vietnam War the town hosted a famous trial involving radical priests. The government accused the priests of plotting to kidnap Henry Kissinger. The trial was a circus. Nancy Downs, herself born a Jew, managed to ingratiate herself with the radical priests. She seduced one of them, convinced him to resign the priesthood so they could marry. They remained married until the former priest was acquitted and the attention blew over. Defrocked, no longer the center of attention, the former priest was now a common man, and Nancy Downs never had a taste for anything common. They divorced. He was ruined. The church wouldn't have him back. He became a blacksmith or something in Kentucky and was never heard from again.

One of my rules of survival therefore was to resist all overtures from Nancy Downs. Not that I really had to. Nancy Downs and I despised each other. She was my nemesis on the editorial board. She never failed to vote against me on whatever matter came up for consideration. She made no secret that she thought me a crude upstart. I made no secret that I thought her a snobbish shrew.

Finally, overriding Nancy Downs' vehement objections, the board sided with me and agreed communal copy editing wasn't working. We broke down and hired yet another editor, this time from out of town, as we didn't trust anyone from our midst. This editor lasted less than a year. His undoing wasn't Nancy Downs, wasn't even his singular professional handicap. He'd been with us nearly six months, editing our copy, when one day he handed someone a sample of his typewriting. He couldn't tell his r's from his w's, his a's from his e's. We'd hired a dyslectic copy editor.

But this as I said didn't lead to his fall. We often hired people with the very infirmities which would prevent them from doing their jobs. It was sort of a hire the handicapped policy. Many of the board members, terrified someone would actually *do* something and upset the status quo, made a point of hiring people unable to do the job. So the copy editor's dyslexia didn't hurt him. What led to his downfall was bringing in the accountant. The new editor's first project had been to recruit a school of business grad who volunteered to go over the books.

The accountant's post opened up after our longtime business manager, Charles "Crackers" McLaughlin, suffered his nervous breakdown. He'd really been holding together very well, all things considered. Then he'd slept with Nancy Downs. Shortly afterwards he was seen hiking down the railroad tracks, a ghetto blaster on his shoulder, screaming along in falsetto with the ever-playing hick radio commercials, "Saturday! Saturday! See nitro-burning funny cars. See hot rod tractors pull each other into fuming piles of rubble and dust! Saturday! Saturday! Golden Grove Speedway. Be there!"

After Crackers ran off we discovered his business practices had been somewhat lax. Crackers didn't exactly follow standard accounting procedures. For a decade, we discovered, he hadn't bothered with such conventions and trivialities as filing local, state or federal taxes. Postal inspectors who every year would be sent to go over our tangled subscriber lists would be thrown into mental derangement and early retirement.

Our lax attitude toward the business side of publishing made our dyslectic editor uneasy. So he brought in the accountant. After a lengthy search we discovered the magazine's business records had been dumped in a dark closet and long forgotten. The business school graduate, an elfin, retiring man named Dave Crispen, disappeared into the the swamp of business records and wasn't seen for eight months. When he finally emerged he sputtered he couldn't understand how the magazine was still running, that it had been operating on what he called "negative cash flow" for most of its existence. By all rights it should have gone out of business years ago, he announced. Everyone on the editorial board just shrugged. Somebody suggested our mistake had been to look into the business records in the first place. Irving Brodsky delivered one of his best lectures on Trotskyism. But the bleak financial report depressed our editor. That night he told the board he was resigning.

"How will you continue?" he wanted to know.

"The same as always," someone replied. It was as good a guess as any.

After the dyslectic editor quit, Dave Crispen, the business school grad, stayed on and joined the board, saying (with the air of a scientist who'd encountered a new form of life) he'd never seen anything like this and wanted to study it further.

I naturally saw this as my big opportunity to become editor. But I was still young and some of the board members, provoked by Nancy Downs, expressed reservations. Then at one board meeting Dave Crispen stood up and said he'd discovered our non-profit status allowed us to apply for government grants. Dave Crispen went ahead and filed a proposal. We promptly were awarded fifty thousand dollars.

Our yearly operating budget had only been twelve thousand. Suddenly we found ourselves with fifty grand. The board, in appreciation, named Dave Crispen the new editor. I felt like quitting.

Dave Crispen unfortunately didn't know much about running a magazine. So the board offered me some of the grant money and gave me the title of news editor. I'd already been scouting around for a reporter's job and had even landed an offer. But I accepted the board's position. I guess I liked that little magazine too much to leave.

Jack Falstaff obviously did too, or he wouldn't have moved in. Falstaff lived in the office for the better part of a year before his luck changed. Someone in his family died and left him a twenty-five thousand dollar inheritance. In one day he blew most of the money. First he bought the rundown row house next to the magazine and began plans for gentrification. Then he went out and bought a brand-new Volvo station wagon. Driving straight from the dealership to a hi-fi store, he bought the most expensive stereo he could find, loading it into the Volvo. Next he went shopping for a sofa. By the time Falstaff got back to his new house, an instant yuppie, he only had a couple grand left.

After he bought his house a disturbed woman moved in with him. I'd be working late at night on a story in the office when I'd hear the two of them yelling at each other through the thin walls. After he'd had the Volvo for about a year she borrowed it one night when she was drunk and tried to drive it up an embankment, blowing out the transmission. Falstaff didn't have the money to fix it so he traded it in for another car, losing thousands of dollars. By this time he'd completely run out of his inheritance. He couldn't even pay his utility bills. Soon his electricity was shut off. He strung an extension cord from his house over to the magazine office, sucking off free electricity.

I guess you could say I was his friend. Jenkins, who worked as a reporter in the capitol newsroom, was his other friend. Jenkins would come over and talk to Falstaff about literature or writing. Me, I'd find myself buttonholed by Falstaff, forced to listen to cruddy football stories. I'd really have no choice about it. He'd crowd himself in the doorway and make it impossible for you to leave.

He had a knack for getting in your way. Just when I'd want to leave the office for the evening I'd hear the front door slam, followed by heavy footsteps coming up the stairs. The stairway boards groaned under his weight. After he'd taken three steps up the stairs always he'd half cough, half clear his throat. I'd brace myself. Why hadn't I left five minutes earlier? Barricading himself in the doorway, he'd subject me to the most mind-numbing hour of long-winded ramblings I'd ever heard in my life.

He'd drive me up the damn wall. He had an innate linebacker's talent for getting in your way. The very moment the idea would cross my mind to wash out my cup I'd find Falstaff on his way over to the sink. Or if I badly had to take a leak, without fail I'd hear Falstaff's heavy feet coming up the stairs, I'd hear that soft cough on the third step, I'd hear him go into the bathroom to take a leisurely half-hour crap while reading the papers.

The day finally came when Falstaff's straits became so dire that he asked me to buy his car so he could pay his gas bill. With winter coming on, he needed money for heat. I heard the heavy footsteps coming up the stairs to my office, heard the soft cough on the third step. I wanted to go to lunch but Falstaff positioned himself in the door, barring my way.

"Ah, Tom! Tom!" His eyes roved around up toward the ceiling like they did when he talked. "Do you want to buy my, ah, car? Only a thousand dollars. It's a, ah, a good deal. I need the money by next week or they'll, ah, shut off my gas."

I'd just received a letter from my friend Nate Freeman asking if I wanted to knock off work for a week and drive out to upper Michigan. Freeman was a good traveling companion. Several years before he'd left his job at the magazine and had since been wandering around the country. At first I'd had no idea why anyone would want to go to upper Michigan but now the idea of taking a long trip seemed appealing.

"I don't know, Falstaff." I pushed past him. "I'm going to lunch. Talk to me about it later."

I managed to avoid Falstaff all week. The day the magazine came back from the printer I got a call from Nate Freeman.

"So let's go to Michigan," he said. "We'll have some kicks. You've got to see the dunes in the upper peninsula."

I wanted to avoid buying Falstaff's car. I stuffed a few copies of the freshly printed magazine into my Boy Scout yucca pack.

"I'm taking next week off," I told Dave Crispen. "Vacation time."

"Where're you going?" He seemed anxious that I was leaving. Rather, anxious I might not come back.

"Michigan."

"Why Michigan?"

"It's a thousand miles away. See you when I get back."

3.

I couldn't wait to get out of the office and walk the ancient miserable cracked brick sidewalks down to the bank. It was a fine day in late July. White clouds floated by in the blue sky above the rounded green mountains. No haze at all. It felt great to be going on vacation. I got my balance from the electronic teat. The little card said I had $1,857.38 in the account. I withdrew three hundred. Then I went home to pack.

I didn't hear from Freeman all night. Not that I expected to. He'd show up at your door in the middle of the night. Something about the night, traveling through it, appealed to him. Looking back, I see my generation hitting the cross-country road at a moment's notice, all the while balancing our Godalmighty careers. A little after midnight the phone rang.

"Hello?"

"I'm just a few miles away. Are you packed?"

"Packed and waiting."

"We'll be over in a while."

"*'We'll'?*"

"Didn't I tell you? John Baines wants to ride along with us as far as Yellow Springs, Ohio. Do you mind?"

Before graduating from college Baines had been an intern at the magazine. Afterwards he'd come back and had been appointed interim editor. He hadn't lasted long. Not that I was surprised. He'd been seduced by Nancy Downs. Shortly afterwards he went nuts, resigned as editor. Nancy Downs no longer had any use for him. But she was the great love of his young life and he hadn't wanted the relationship to end.

Nancy Downs had had to go to great lengths to extricate herself from the relationship. She went so far as to drive him down to New Orleans, where he'd landed a job with a daily newspaper. She dumped him off and drove home as fast as she could. But within the month Baines quit the newspaper job and came back to town in a last-ditch attempt to patch things up. It had gone badly. She got frank with him. It ended with her throwing him out of her apartment.

The day she threw him out I was at the office. Baines came in, wild-eyed and shaken. He stood in the middle of the floor, eyeing the cluttered bulletin board. No one ever cleaned the bulletin board. Notices dating back to the Vietnam War hung on the board. It was a memorandum board for our age. Baines stood there kind of shaking. He announced he was going to clean off the bulletin board. He dug into it. Papers and dust flew. Shortly thereafter he'd gone completely off the deep end.

He went off the deep end in ways I won't go in to here. The important thing is that afterwards I had two rules of survival: Don't sleep with Nancy Downs. And never clean off the bulletin board.

So now Baines was bailing out and leaving town altogether. He wanted to ride with us as far as his old college campus in Ohio.

"I don't mind. Baines's all right, I guess."

"Well we'll be around before too long."

Hours passed. A little after three in the morning Freeman's car pulled up. He got out of the car with Baines.

"What took you so long?"

"I had to write a note to this *beautiful* woman I just met."

In those days Freeman floated like a bee from one women to the next. They could never figure him out. The first time I met him he had two women in tow. This was years before, when I'd first started at the magazine. He'd stopped by the office on his way to a concert he was reviewing. He'd had these two befuddled women along with him to help take notes and photographs.

"It sure took you long enough," I told him.

"Tell me about it!" Baines whined. His patience already had been tested. "We're taking too damn long to get on the road. It's nearly three in the morning! Who ever heard of going anywhere at three in the morning? I have to be at Yellow Springs, Ohio by seven o'clock tonight."

"Relax," Freeman told him. "We'll get there by seven o'clock tonight. It's only four or five hundred miles."

We started carrying my things out to the car. It was so late a police car stopped. The cop got out of his cruiser. I had to show him ID to convince him I wasn't looting my own place. In the end the cop wished me a nice time and drove off.

It was almost four before we got on the road. Freeman took a roundabout route.

"Where're we going?" Baines wanted to know. "This isn't the way to the turnpike."

"I'm dropping this note off at this woman's house."

"Aw for christsakes Freeman! I've got to be in Yellow Springs, Ohio by seven o'clock this evening!"

"Is this how it's going to be the whole way? If it is you can take the bus."

Baines shut up. Before long Freeman parked the car in front of a mobile home. We were somewhere in the middle of the dark countryside.

"Have you ever met this woman?" Freeman pointed at the

darkened trailer. "I think she's the most beautiful woman in the world."

It was really too dark to see anything.

"So you're in love now, are you?"

"This woman's beautiful enough to be in love with."

He got out of the car and hurried off into the night, around to the side of the mobile home, leaving his note in her milk box. Baines grumbled the whole time. Freeman came back to the car and, wanting to needle Baines, made it a point to take the back roads all the way to Pittsburgh. He took Route 22 the whole way. I hadn't slept all night so when the conversation slacked off I passed out in the backseat. I must've slept for hours. When I opened my eyes the sun was up. We were going over the Alleghenies. Lying there on the seat I watched the trees go by. The engine of the car strained. When we made it to the top of the range Freeman pulled into a park, shut off the ignition.

"Why're we stopping here?"

"This is the Allegheny Portage Railroad. I have to check something out."

Freeman was working on a novel about a young couple who were pursuing a UFO around the national park system. He had a room at his parents' house but lately he'd been traveling all around the country researching his book, stopping at every imaginable public monument. He'd become a walking encyclopedia of forgotten American monuments. I was once with him when he visited an absurd monument to President McKinley at the Antietam civil war battlefield. As a young man McKinley had served coffee to the troops during the battle. His statue at Antietam shows the future president holding a pot of coffee.

In recent years Freeman had done most of his travel by hitchhiking. He'd once hitched for days to a friend's house in California, outside LA, only to discover that the friend had moved to Mexico the week before. A cocktail waitress now lived in the apartment. The cocktail waitress had come home in the middle of the night to find Freeman and his backpack on her doorstep. She'd let him in to spend the night on the living room floor. They'd spent the next day together. He even met her at work later that night and went home with her again. Nothing happened. Perhaps because nothing happened she told him this arrangement wasn't working and he'd have to hit the road. So he left the next day, heading east. In Colorado he caught a ride from a young couple who told him they had a close friend in Kansas named Jane Rae, who they called Janer, and if ever he was passing through Salina, Kansas he should look her up, as they were sure he would like her, so he made a note. He was always taking copious notes.

By chance, Freeman claims, the next day found him passing through Salina. He went to the address on the note, an apartment building. Janer wasn't home. He waited out in the parking lot, watching women go by — older women, heavyset women with little children. Finally a young woman fitting Janer's description showed up. He introduced himself. They hit it off right away. She wanted to know how her friends were doing. She took him into her apartment and made dinner. She had all the right books and records. It turned out she worked in a small planetarium in town. She let him spend the night on her floor.

The next day he walked into town and visited her at the planetarium. They made a date to drive into Wichita that night in her pickup. She had some things to pick up for the planetarium. They spent a nice evening in Wichita. Driving home, they agreed he'd be gone the next day. The next day came and she went to work. He hung out in her apartment all day reading her books, listening to her records, passing the day idly, when suddenly he looked up and saw it was almost five o'clock and she'd be home any minute. He furiously threw his things into his pack and hit the road, not wanting to break his promise.

Another time, somewhere in the Midwest, Freeman, hungry and down on his luck, met a man who bragged that he'd trained his house cat to steal meat from the neighborhood supermarket. No sooner had the man gone off when Freeman spied a tabby hauling a cellophane-wrapped package of ground chuck. He chased after the cat, which was much slowed by its burden. Grabbing the package, Freeman tore off a corner with fang marks and returned the morsel inside to the feline. Then he made a fire and cooked hamburgers, the whole time watched by the cat.

Not that all his adventures were so cordial. One day in his travels he met a young woman who invited him to stay the night at her parents' house. Her father, it turned out, recently had retired from IBM as a senior vice president. This go-getting captain of industry instantly disliked Freeman's lazy vagabond lifestyle. Though the family kept a guesthouse, the retired IBM executive refused to give Freeman a comfortable night's lodging. The guesthouse was too good for an itinerant writer. The old man would only allow Nate to unroll his sleeping bag on the floor of the den.

At seven-thirty the next morning, a Saturday, the retired executive woke Freeman, telling him to get up, that breakfast was ready and nobody slept past seven in *his* household. Besides, the retired executive said, he had pressing business to conduct in the den. The retired executive then got on the phone and started making business calls. Freeman sleepily gathered up his things. Never a breakfast eater, Nate decided to skip the morning meal and hit the road early. He left the house as breakfast was put on the table. This lapse of manners so infuriated the retired IBM executive that the old man slammed down the phone and came running from the house after Freeman, yelling, "Next time why don't you call ahead with your reservations so we can have accommodations waiting the way you like them!" Freeman's travels had given him a hundred stories like that.

Now, at the Portage Railroad, after shuffling around in his backpack to make sure he had his notepad and camera, he got out of the car. Baines stayed behind. I followed Freeman up the trail to the visitors' center. It was still too early in the morning. The place was closed. We had to wait another forty-five minutes for the rangers to show up. A spring babbled out of the woods and we killed time poking around the water. Looking down through the trees we saw Baines get out of the car. He started kicking a Park Service picnic table.

"It doesn't look like Baines appreciates the Portage Railroad."

"Why'd you bring him along, anyway?"

"I didn't think he'd be this bad."

"Why does he have to be in Yellow Springs, Ohio tonight?"

"Search me."

Baines quit kicking the picnic table. He started walking up the trail through the trees. He came across the clearing with his hands in his pockets. His beard was all mussed up.

"Nate, what are we doing?"

"Relax. It'll open in another twenty minutes or so."

"Nate you know I really *do* have to be in Yellow Springs, Ohio by seven o'clock this evening."

"I know, I know. If it looks like you won't make it we'll put you on the bus in Pittsburgh."

Baines sat down on a pile of rocks beside the spring. We didn't have long to wait. An old park ranger hobbled bent-backed out of a trailer at the edge of the clearing. With early morning weariness he padded up the trail to the visitors' center. We followed him in. He ushered us into a small viewing room. A portrait of the president of the United States hung on the back wall. The old man started a film about the Portage Railroad. Baines wasn't enthusiastic. He impatiently watched the film, shifting in his seat. He didn't get his way all day. After we left the Portage Railroad Freeman insisted on making more ridiculous stops.

"America is a country of travelers, with monuments to travelers," Freeman lectured as he zoomed over the mountains. "Our religion is travel. Notice we don't build towering cathedrals to God. We build ornate train depots like Grand Central Station, rocket assembly buildings towering to the sky. Cathedrals to travel. The portage railroad is a monument to travelers of the old canals. They wanted to get over the mountains to the Ohio and Mississippi River valleys. The Horseshoe Curve was built by travelers trying to get over the same mountains by train. Since you two are so obviously interested I see I should definitely take you to see the Horseshoe Curve."

But first, to underscore his point, we stopped at a ridiculous monument to American traveler Admiral Peary. The admiral was ensconced in a granite parka with a granite husky by his side. Then it was on to the Horseshoe Curve, then Johnstown. Baines almost lost his mind at the monument to Admiral Peary.

"Why build monuments when people are in too much of a furious rush to stop?" Freeman sighed.

Baines finally resigned himself to the stops. At the Horseshoe Curve the three of us killed time waiting for a train. The track followed a curving path inside a great ravine. There was nothing. We were about to leave when, in the distance, a whistle sounded. A train came round. It took ten minutes for the engine to thread its way all the way down to the bottom. You could see the whole length of the mile-long train going around the curve. From there we drove to the Johnstown dam, scene of the famous catastrophe. The whole while Freeman narrated the disaster.

"The dam had been built by wealthy nineteenth-century Pittsburgh industrialists who wanted to make a recreational lake for their sporting club. The wealthy industrialists hadn't properly maintained the dam. You know what they say: private mismanagement, public disaster. The day the dam broke no one believed warnings about the wall of water that was racing down the mountain." Reading from his notes, Freeman recited an old folk song which mentions a stranger who came running into Johnstown warning of the disaster, but since the locals didn't know the stranger they paid him no heed.

By the time we got to the broken dam in Johnstown Baines let loose enough to skip a few stones in the spilled reservoir. He'd realized he couldn't influence our lazy schedule so he might as well enjoy himself as best he could. By noon we were on the road again, this time heading southwest.

When we reached Ohio Freeman, yawning, climbed into the backseat to sleep. I took the wheel. It was a straight road through green farm country. I drove like a maniac, racing past brightly colored fields until they blurred like an expressionist painting. Patches of green bean fields, waving corn, sudden explosions of yellow sunflowers. Old Gothic farmhouses, painted white and heavy with age, whizzed by.

I passed the time listening to Baines talk about his new girl. Hoping to get Nancy Downs out of his mind he'd done the wise thing and found someone new. He thought the world of his new girl. He'd go on and on about her. A month earlier, Baines had introduced me to her. We'd been out drinking. She'd been sitting on Baines' lap, all smiles, when she shook my hand. Afterwards I walked across the crowded bar and ran into my friend Mike. The same woman now sat on Mike's lap. Mike introduced her to me as *his* new girl. Again we shook hands. I thought I'd been a study of cordiality. At the time I'd wanted to stay out of it. Now, driving across Ohio, listening to Baines go on and on about what a wonderful, true woman she was, I couldn't take anymore. I didn't believe in love, I guess. Maybe I just had too much time to kill.

I told Baines I'd seen his wonderful true woman on Mike's

lap on the other side of the bar. Freeman sat up in the backseat and howled with laughter. Baines couldn't believe it. He said he'd write her as soon as he got to Yellow Springs.

"Aw don't go writing any letters," I told him. Already I was sorry I'd said anything.

At least it shut Baines up. We made good time across Ohio. We'd nearly reached Yellow Springs when Freeman insisted on stopping at an ancient Indian burial grounds. Baines impatiently followed us around a field of mysterious mounds. We spent an agonizingly long time investigating. The entire broad field was dotted with mounds.

"This is like being inside a pinball machine."

"They're burial mounds," Freeman explained. "If you excavated them you'd find bones."

"How old are they?"

"No one knows. Several thousand years anyway."

"That old?"

One of the mounds had been cut open by the Park Service and encased in glass so tourists could get a glimpse of ancient Indian burial rituals. The interior of the mound was all lit up with fluorescent lights, which hung down everywhere inside the mound. We pressed against the plate glass, looking inside, seeing the white bones neatly spread out among shards of painted pottery and trinkets.

"Fluorescent lights, very nice. These Indians *were* advanced."

At last we got back into the car and drove the few remaining miles into Yellow Springs. It was a little after six in the evening. Baines wasted no time. We dropped him off at the main green of his alma mater. He hurried away across campus, barely bothering to say good-bye.

"Must be in a hurry for something," Freeman said.

While we were there we figured we might as well look up a few friends. Interns who'd worked at the magazine. We walked around the dorms but no one was in. I suggested we grab a bite.

"I've got trail mix in the car," Freeman said.

"I need more than bird seed. How about some real food?"

We drove through a stand of tall brooding trees into the little college town, going into the first place we saw. It was a little after seven. At the counter, eating the blue-plate special, sat Baines.

"Well look who it is."

Baines seemed depressed. He didn't even notice when we sat down beside him.

"Don't tell us you had to be here at seven o'clock so you could eat the hash and beans," Freeman said.

Baines listlessly looked up.

"Oh hello guys."

"What's the matter, John?"

"This place has changed so much. Nobody I know is here anymore."

An old black woman worked behind the counter. She came over for our order. Baines asked hopefully if she remembered him. You could tell she didn't know him. But countless encounters with lost alumni had taught her how to respond. A flash of recognition lit her face.

"Why, yes yes," she said, eyeing Baines from each side. "I think I do remember you."

Baines looked pleased.

It fueled her on.

"You didn't have that beard when you were here, did you, honey?"

"Yes, I've always had this beard."

She went away with our order.

"Don't be too disappointed, Baines."

"I'm not disappointed. It's just all these new faces. New professors. You'd think some things wouldn't change but then you go there and you see they have."

Baines really didn't have any place special to be at seven. We felt sorry for him. The three of us left the diner together for the student dorms. This time one of our friends was there. Maggie Whitman came running from her room. She threw her arms around Freeman and me. She was a nice young thang from Atlanta who'd been an intern at the magazine the year before.

"Why Tom!" She had a marvelous Southern drawl. "How nice to see y'all!"

It turned out she had a date that night with some guy who'd promised to teach her to play the drums. She took all three of us along. What a sweet girl. The drummer didn't know what to think when the three of us showed up with his date. The whole night he kept trying to make time with Maggie while Freeman and Baines pounded wildly away on his bongo drums in the living room. Finally, around midnight, the drummer suggested we all go out for pizza. The five of us left together. We hadn't taken ten steps from his door when the drummer suddenly stopped, saying he'd forgotten something. We should go on without him, he suggested. He'd catch up with us later at the pizza parlor. We never saw him again.

I was much too tired to go for pizza. I begged off. I plodded alone down the dark muddy streets back to Maggie's dorm but I'd forgotten to ask for the key to her room. I ended up pulling my sleeping bag from Freeman's car and crashing in the grass.

4.

In the morning I woke up all covered with dew. I brushed off the cold sparkle and went into Maggie's dorm. Freeman and Baines had camped out on her floor. They were just getting out of their sleeping bags.

"Tom, where were you?" Maggie crooned when I came in. She was stretching in her bed. "I was looking for you last night."

The four of us walked over to the cafeteria and ate breakfast on her food card. She insisted. I had eggs, a stale Danish and some coffee. After breakfast Freeman and I said good-bye to Maggie and Baines. We watched them wave as we rolled away. A whole day of driving stretched ahead of us. Freeman careened up one back road and down another. I sat back and watched the window music. In beautiful rolling country we stopped at a tourist cavern. They were running boats through the cave. The lines were too long so we didn't take a boat. We hopped back in the car and took off. Freeman insisted on stopping at a little town called Bellefontaine.

"America's first concrete street was laid out around Bellefontaine's courthouse," he explained.

"They probably had the first potholes, too."

We hung around the courthouse for an interminably long time. Freeman made a big deal of it. I hung in the background, under a shade tree, watching Freeman, a bundle of energy. All around the courthouse he ran, taking pictures. He ran down the block to a Woolworth's to buy souvenirs of the crumbling concrete street. He came out with a pack of postcards, all excited.

"Man! I just saw the most *beautiful* woman in the world. Working at the counter of the five and dime back there. I bought some penny candy from her."

The scenery became one moving picture of towns and farmland, blue sky and interstate. We stopped at Ann Arbor and I showed Freeman where I'd once lived (for a summer when I was seventeen) in the office of the famous Human Rights Party, which had legalized marijuana. I took him to a restaurant run by hippies who made the best chapaties I've ever eaten, but the place was closed.

"Now I feel like Baines," I said, staring through the darkened window.

"Come on. We have to be in Yellow Springs, Ohio by seven o'clock tonight."

We hit the road again without eating, heading north. In Flint we stopped for gas. An old man, seeing our license plate, volunteered that he held a warm place in his heart for Easterners. "You have well-mannered coloreds back there in the East," he told us. He launched into a tirade about how America was going to hell. "Look what they did to Nixon!" he told us. "Those bastards forced him to resign! Without so much as a trial. My idea is that they should have administered a truth sermon to Nixon. And whatever he said they should've been forced to abide by it, until the statue of limitations ran out."

We said good-bye to the old man and drove off. The sun was going down. I pulled out my pipe, propped my feet on the dash.

Freeman started complaining.
"Why do you have to smoke that thing? What if we get pulled over? This is my mother's car, you know."
I felt like Huck Finn. We were going over the boundless interstate at a fast clip, heading into the red sunset.
"What do you think?" I said. "Maybe Kerouac once came down this road."
"Did I ever tell you I met him?" Freeman asked.
"You met Kerouac?"
He lifted his eyebrows and bit his lower lip, making his black beard hairs stand away from his chin, like he always did when he knew he had your attention. He was driving furiously down the road.
"Didn't I ever tell you? It was back in the sixties, when I was in college. We had this failed writer as head of our English Department. Before he'd taken his chair he'd published several literary novels in New York City. They'd been well received in the literary community but they'd only sold maybe a few thousand copies each."
"So he was no big deal."
"Right, he was no big deal. So he did the logical thing. He took the job as head of the English Department at my school. Out in the middle of nowhere he could be the big man on campus."
"Big fish in a small pond kind of thing."
"Exactly. He'd host these parties where he'd sit around all night talking about Roth, Updike, Bellow and himself. One weekend I was hitching back to campus to go to one of his parties. I was on the side of the road when a big black fifties Hudson pulled over. There were two guys in front. We'd hardly pulled off when the one in the passenger's seat starts telling me he's Neil Cassidy."
"Was he?"
"I told him I didn't believe it. He got all excited then and

said well maybe he wasn't Cassidy but the one behind the wheel was Jack Kerouac. I didn't believe that either. So the one behind the wheel gets all excited. 'I *am* Kerouac!' he yelled. He pulled out his driver's license and threw it to the backseat. I nearly died. He was Jack Kerouac! It turned out he was driving the Hudson up from Florida for a friend. He liked picking up hitchhikers. He'd picked up the guy in the front seat and he'd picked up me."

"So you met Kerouac? What was he like?"

"He was a nice guy. Very warm. Likeable. Very open. He had this sort of grin that told you he thought he was getting away with things. You would have liked him."

"I'm sure. What happened?"

"What do you do when you find yourself speeding down the road with Jack Kerouac? I told him there was a party on campus and asked him to come. Man, when I walked into that party with Jack Kerouac! All of a sudden this sleepy little party comes alive when they find out who's in the room."

"They knew who he was?"

"Are you kidding? This was at the height of his fame. They engulfed him. Believe me, the last person the failed writer who was head of the English Department expected to come through his door was Jack Kerouac. All night he and Kerouac were like opposing poles on a magnet, circling each other, not speaking. Finally they got pushed together and the prof laid into the beat. Didn't he know he was poisoning these young impressionable minds? What was the idea of passing that rubbish off as literature? Kerouac got all quiet. Then he flew into this thing about the north wind blowing down cold over the plains or some pseudo zen bit like that. It was amazing. The minute before he'd been enthusiastically talking with us about football and cars and music and Neil Cassidy. Confronted with criticism, he flew into this ridiculous inaccessible rap that made no sense at all. Then he turned and stormed from the party. We were left to wonder where Kerouac went when he became inaccessible."

That night we camped in a state forest. The campground was closed for the night but we went in anyway. We drove around until we found a campsite that suited us. We parked and hiked back to the forester's office, leaving a couple dollars in a can that had been nailed to a tree. There was barely enough light for us to find wood. Still I was insistent on building a fire.

It turned out Freeman had visited this same campground, years before, with an old girlfriend.

"I spent that summer traveling all around the country with her," he told me, poking the fire. "She has this van that she bought from an electrical contractor. On its side he'd painted the words 'You phone us, we'll wire you.' We traveled all around, sleeping in the van. It was great."

"What happened to her?"

"After we finished traveling we shared an apartment. Then one day a friend of mine came to visit. She fell in love with him."

"How'd that happen?"

"I was too busy playing basketball to see what was going on, I guess. She came home one afternoon and kicked me out."

"What'd she say?"

"Only that she was taking up with my friend. It came as quite a blow. Screw," he poked in the fire, "sex is boring anyway."

"That's right. It's just another dull physical activity."

"Physical? That's where you're wrong. It's mostly mental."

A little after midnight a car pulled into the next campsite over. A man and a woman got out and scrounged for firewood. They tripped through the dark woods, breaking sticks and rustling leaves. Soon they'd started their own little fire. There we were, out in the middle of nowhere, two solitary campfires blazing, two solitary camps without contact. Before long I took my ensolite and sleeping bag from the car, unrolled them on the ground by the fire. I slept well. In the morning when I awoke the man and the woman in the next campsite were already gone. Freeman crawled out of his sleeping bag, complaining his back was stiff. He hadn't any ensolite and had slept on the cold hard ground. He walked around holding his back, complaining.

"I used to be able to sleep on the ground. I must be getting old."

We were on the road before nine. Driving north, we could look out through the trees. Now and then we'd see swatches of Lake Huron on the right, Lake Michigan on the left. When we got to the top of the peninsula Freeman insisted on stopping at a tourist trap which claimed to possess the world's largest crucifix. It must have been a hundred feet tall. A plaque read that the giant crucifix had been built as a monument to a frontier Indian girl whose name had been Kateri Tekakwitha, or Lily of the Mohawks. Long ago she had wandered all around creation leaving small crosses in the woods. Sad men and women were being pushed in wheelchairs to the foot of the giant cross to pray. A few weeks earlier the pope had died in Rome and a priest now stood at a giant altar up front offering prayers to his successor. Out of habit I dipped my hand in a trough of holy water.

We blew an entire hour at the giant crucifix. From there Freeman drove directly to another tourist trap called Sea Shell City.

"You have to see this place! You won't believe it!"

Inside he showed me a clear acrylic toilet seat that had samples of barbed wire set into it. While he dug through the junk in Sea Shell City I went outside. I relaxed in the grass off to the side of the parking lot. A dairy farm sat on a hill next to the tourist trap. An electric fence, keeping in the cows, hemmed the edge of the parking lot. I went over to the fence, listening to the current crackling through the wires. Just for kicks I touched a wire. I got a hell of a jolt. I don't know what I'd expected.

Freeman came out from Sea Shell City all loaded down with postcards. We took the car over the Mackinac Bridge. You could look out over the water and see all the barges slowly plying the still lakes. When we came off the bridge we were in the woods of upper Michigan. Finally we'd reached wilderness. We drove a hundred miles through thick forest, seeing few cars. You could smell water through the trees. When we came out of the trees at Grand Marais there was Lake Superior, deep and steel gray, dead ahead. We stopped at a little store to buy a week's worth of groceries. I bought a gallon jug of red wine. Then we drove along the shore to Pictured Rocks.

We came down through thick stands of white birch, taking a big, wooded campsite near the shore. I hadn't taken ten steps from the car when, looking down, I spotted a 35mm film canister at my feet. Scooping it up, I saw it was half filled with what looked like fine Jamaican.

"Well how about that! What luck!"

Feeling pretty good, I walked with Freeman along the lakeshore for a bit, climbing and jumping down great dunes and cliffs of white sand. Already the sun was starting down. I wanted to get back to our campsite to gather wood. Freeman would have no part of it. He couldn't see building campfires.

"Why do you always have to be gathering wood? I've got a primus."

"It's not the same. You can't sit around a primus."

We walked back along the beach to the campsite. Freeman sat ribbing me while I thrashed about the woods gathering sticks.

"It's my gathering instinct," I yelled back through the woods.

I built a nice fire. We cooked dinner over it. While we ate, a burly man in a four-wheel drive truck took the next campsite. He set up a four-man tent, then one of those big camp stoves. From the back of his truck he took two folding chairs and a guitar. Finally he carried a retarded boy down from the truck to the campsite. Well into the night the burly man sat tenderly playing the guitar and singing to the retarded boy.

After it was dark I followed Freeman down to the sand cliffs overlooking the shore. We could hear the big man singing. Somewhere on the far side of the immense dark cold lake was Canada. I had my wine and my pipe. Freeman even took a tentative sip at the bottle. He didn't like it. He couldn't see why anyone would want to drink or smoke. His vice was that he didn't have any. He threw the bottle back down to the sand. We sat on the sand cliffs looking out over the deep imponderable inland sea. The sky blazed with stars.

"You know what? I think the constellations in the sky should be renamed after Americans."

"How do you mean?"

"Instead of Leo, Orion and the Big Dipper we could redraw the constellations, naming them after twentieth-century American icons. Mickey Mouse. Dick Nixon. Marilyn Monroe."

"Instead of the Seven Sisters we'd have the Seven Dwarfs?"

"It'd give a whole new meaning to the planet Pluto, wouldn't it?"

Freeman's attention suddenly was drawn high overhead.

"Would you look at that."

He pointed practically straight up. The northern lights poured down from the top of the sky, falling like a shimmering white curtain nearly all the way down to the horizon. Its reflection on the water made the lake look like it was on fire.

The next five days I mostly did nothing but drink. I tried swimming in the lake but even in late summer it was too cold for anything but a brief dunk. I waded in and took a dive, swimming a few feet down to the sandy bottom, stirring up the sand in the murky water. Surfacing, I rolled over and did a few strokes on my back, blowing water from my mouth, but it was just too cold to be much fun. I came out and stood shivering on the beach. I took to keeping the wine cold by jamming the bottle in the rocks along the shore. After the bottle started getting empty I had to weigh it down with rocks to keep it from floating away.

Freeman had brought along a portable typewriter. Each morning he'd disappear into the dunes to work on his novel. I'd also brought along a little portable. One afternoon both of us were sitting along the sand cliffs typing away when a middle-aged couple on vacation came hiking by. They were surprised to see us typing furiously on the dunes. The old couple seemed most impressed by Freeman. The woman said she'd never seen a novelist at work before.

"And you?" the woman asked me. "Are you working on a novel too?"

"Fat chance," I said. "I'm working on this bottle of wine."

"He's a writer too," Freeman told the lady.

I rooted around in my yucca pack and gave them a fresh copy of the magazine. The cover story concerned a fictitious meltdown at a nuclear plant near our hometown.

They seemed interested so I told them how the article came to be written. My first act as news editor had been to ask the local anti-nukes for the name of someone who could write an article about a hypothetical meltdown at the nuclear power plant. I thought it'd make a nice story. They referred me to a man named Lenny Popadopolis. I phoned this guy and asked him to stop by the office for a chat. Lenny Popadopolis turned out to be a long-haired holdover hippie whose self-described area of expertise was paranormal psychic phenomena and spontaneous human combustion.

"What sort of article would you have us write?" he asked

when he came in. For some reason he always referred to himself in the plural.

"Describe an accident at the nuclear power plant," I told him.

"How bad an accident should we write about?"

I was in a bad mood.

"Pull out all the damn stops. Make it the worst possible accident you can imagine."

The psychic phenomena expert seemed startled.

"We believe that would be a class nine nuclear accident," he said quietly. "A meltdown."

"Very well," I told him. "Get on with it then."

Now the woman in Michigan thanked me half-heartedly for the copy of the magazine. Probably thinking I was nuts, she walked away stuffing it into her purse. I remember how lost I felt. My life was going nowhere.

The next day I was hiking through the woods when a little dog came running down the trail, chased by two young men. I never much cared for dogs, and I almost let this one pass, but at the last moment I stuck out my leg, barring its way. I helped them catch their dog. They were so grateful they had me back to their camp for lunch. An odd trailer was hitched behind their car.

"It's a hangglider," one of them said.

"Ever been hanggliding?" the other asked.

"Me? I'd probably kill myself."

The one kept saying "shit."

"Shit. You have to give it a try."

I wasn't sure. They wouldn't take no for an answer.

"Shit, no."

They'd come to hurl themselves off the high sand cliffs but I wouldn't have any part of that. They agreed the dunes might make a safer place for my maiden flight. So we lugged the glider down to the rolling sand along the shore. We carried it up the largest dune. The rainbow-colored fabric snapped and hummed in the breeze. It seemed to want to lunge into the air. I was beginning to have serious reservations. I hmmed and hahhed that maybe this wasn't such a good idea. They wouldn't hear of it. "Shit, we can't let you off that easy." They strapped me into the harness.

"Shit, whatever you do, don't let go. Hold on tight to the bar."

"Believe me I have no intention of letting go."

I was pointed into the wind. Already I could feel my feet lifting from the sand. The men held on to my shirt.

"I don't know about this. Look what happened to Icarus."

"Shit, Icarus was a wimp. And he didn't follow instructions."

"There's nothing to worry about."

"Just don't fly too far over the water, that's sure as shit."

"Believe me, I have no intention of doing that."

"And don't try flying straight into the wind at takeoff. That's a good way to kill yourself and shit. A common mistake made by beginners. You won't have enough air speed and you'll stall. The wind might flip you over backwards. You could get hurt. Break your neck and shit. Try flying down the side of the dune to pick up speed. Then, when you're near the bottom, push out on the bar. You'll be flying. Use your weight to steer, like a bicycle. Follow the beach and you'll probably hit an updraft."

"I hope that's all I hit."

I hesitated. The bar felt clammy in my hands. The hot breeze stiffened in my face.

"I don't know about this."

"Now!"

They let go of my shirt. I pushed off, my feet dragging across the sand. I followed the contour of the dune down toward the shore, seeing the lake rush up. Man was I picking up speed! My feet no longer scraped the sand. I was running out of dune.

"Push! Push!" I heard one of them yell. I pushed out on the bar and the yellow sand rushed away beneath me. I was climbing, my feet stretched out behind, my arms outstretched in front. Over the dunes I sailed, the world falling away. I've always wanted to be free of the world and for an instant I thought I'd succeeded. Then — a swatch of blue. I hadn't watched where I'd been going. Now I was a good fifty feet over the lake. It was ghostly quiet up there. Far out on the water I could see a freighter peacefully crawling. Closer in, a fish jumped. I thought, This must be how an angel feels looking down from heaven.

Someone behind me yelled, "Bring it around! Bring it around!" Bearing my weight to the left, I came around, but lost altitude fast. It must have looked like I was taking a nose dive into the drink because I heard one last loud "Shit!" The two of them, looks of calamity in their faces, came barreling over the dunes. I swooped down low over the beach and made a clumsy landing in the sand. Bending low to catch my breath, I unsnapped the harness as the two of them came running up.

Two days later I was exploring the dunes when I looked out over the water and saw Freeman swimming naked in the lake. He'd just finished his book and was immersing himself in the water. As for me, I'd finished the bottle of wine that morning and had just buried it deep in the sand. It was time to go home.

The ride back was quiet. We listened to the radio. On our way through Detroit, as the Bee Gees were singing Staying Alive, an announcer broke in with a special news bulletin. The pope was dead. Then he returned us to Staying Alive.

"Did he say the pope's dead?"

"I thought the pope already was dead."

"It must be the new pope. That little guy. Pope John Paul.

He didn't last long, did he?"

"Those bishops must've bumped him off."

On a curving two-lane road we whipped past an ancient man with a long white beard who sat rocking on a shady porch.

"Bet he thinks Eisenhower's still president."

We took a northern route across Ohio, stopping at Kent State to look at the field where the four students had been shot by the National Guard. I took a whiz on an administration building they were erecting on the site.

"Nixon should have come here and made a speech, like the Gettysburg Address," I told Freeman. "Maybe then things might've come out all right."

"What a stupid idea," Freeman said. We argued about it. We were starting to get on each other's nerves.

At last we hit Route 80. A little after nightfall we reached the Pennsylvania border. We came down through State College, listening to country music on the radio. It was almost three in the morning when we got home. I had Freeman swing by the office so I could get my mail.

In the office at three that morning I heard the front door slam. I heard the three heavy steps, followed by the cough.

Falstaff came excitedly up the steps.

"Tom! Tom! Where've you been, buddy? You promised you'd buy my car. I need the money first thing this morning or they'll, ah, shut off my gas!"

5.

Several auspicious things happened the week after I got back from my vacation. I bought Falstaff's car. He hounded me so much I finally broke down and bought it. For the longest time I'd been riding city buses around town. I bought Falstaff's car not so much because I wanted to do him any favors but because I was sick of riding the bus.

It was the second car I'd ever owned. I used to own a 1966 Volkswagen Squareback. But it kept popping its hood at freeway speeds. In the end my Volkswagen was spread all along the road. I'd become one of many people who'd ride a mass transit bus.

The TV ads for riding the bus made it seem like a romantic experience. On a bright and sunny day, standing at a clean bus stop, a well-dressed businessman tells you he enjoys riding the bus, chatting with new friends on his way up to the community college to study Spanish. Somewhere off the television screen a chorus is mindlessly singing, "Hey, there, welcome aboard, let's ride the bus." The man proudly tells you he's a mass transit rider. I never saw that man on a bus, but I did witness Puerto Ricans riding out from the barrios to study English.

Riding the bus was not always devil may care. One day a police car pulled in front of our silver and orange diesel chariot, and two cops informed us a lady had just been mugged somewhere near the high school. The culprits, we were told, had hopped our bus and we were all suspects. Everyone on the bus fit the description. All twenty of us. In the end the cops left empty-handed, taking only our time. The way I used to hang around city street corners you'd think I had nothing but time.

I had a favorite place where I liked to sit when I did my mass transit thing. Near the back. I didn't say much, usually. I liked to listen to what the other mass transit riders had to say.

One day two old men, Charlie and George, both laborer types, became engaged in conversation.

"Well, Charlie," said George, "I've just been married. Got this woman that'll take good care of me and fix m'meals. Yes sir."

"What ya gonna do with a woman, George?" asked the other. "Yer too old a cuss for that stuff, George."

George said nothing. He smiled. Charlie seemed to become angry. He was old and unmarried and those things tend to hang on a mass transit rider like barnacles on a ship. Charlie thought.

"Yes sir," said George.

Charlie said this country had gone to hell. He said our constitution was no good and we ought to overthrow the government. Revolutionary fervor on a bus.

The other man looked shocked.

"Now, you shouldn't speak out against the government, Charlie. Mmm, mmm. Ain't no good comin' from that kinda talk!"

Charlie continued. Castro could teach us a thing or two, Charlie went on.

"We oughta get rid of them guys in Washington and bring up Castro from Cuber."

Infuriated, George said, "Now, this woman's takin'

goooooood care of me."

"I hear ya."

George pulled the cord and stormed off the bus. Take care, George, and we rolled on.

Shortly after I returned from vacation I met the love of my life on a mass transit bus. She seemed to have the body of Bardot and the mind of Einstein. Or maybe I'd just been standing in the sun too long, waiting for the bus. I quickly found myself sitting next to her, flipping out, wracking my mind to think of a place in the city where I could meet her later. Her name was Karen.

Every nook and cranny in town flashed through my mind. I was crazy. I thought of the corny solar system display on the third floor of the museum. I became another mass transit orator.

"Meet me in front of the elephant bones on the third floor of the museum," I said.

She giggled. She wondered. The other mass transit riders listened to my spiel. I got some sort of a commitment from her to meet me there, and she pulled the cord to get off. Karen said after we met at the elephant bones she could give me a ride home *in her car*. At last, I thought, I'd be graduating from the bus.

I had selected an out-of-the-ordinary place like the museum's elephant bones because I wanted her to know how unusual she was to me. At the appointed time I found myself in front of the elephant bones. A plaque on the wall proclaimed the skeleton to be "The Marshall's Creek Mastodon," found in a peat bog somewhere in Pennsylvania in the sixties. No one knows for sure what killed off the species of Pennsylvania elephants.

Karen never showed up. I felt like shit. Standing on the third floor of the museum, in front of the goddamn elephant bones, I finally figured out what killed off the Marshall's Creek

Mastodon. If that poor creature had been alive today I swear he would have been a mass transit bus rider.

Well, at least I still had ninety-five cents in exact change, and the Third Street bus was hardly ever more than three hours away. Hey, there, welcome aboard.

I got on the bus with a woman with fire-red hair. We sat toward the back, and she proceeded to tell her story to no one in particular. She said she had a baby. At first, she said, she thought it would be a drag "but I just decided I wanted to have this baby, and that it could be a joy, and I had the baby and it was a joy. Everything's in your mind," she said.

She said she danced on tables in night clubs in Florida, and was passing through town. She hoped she wasn't offending anyone, she said, but "this town has a reputation up and down the coast as a gay city." The trouble with this place, she suggested, was that most of the men were gay.

"For instance," she said, "and I hope I don't offend the guy, but I can tell that guy's gay."

She pointed to a man sitting toward the front. She said she knew the man's sexual preferences because he had his hair cut above his ears, "and everybody knows that men who show their ears these days are gay."

The guy with the exposed ears froze. Everyone stared at him. A fellow mass transit rider who sat next to him slyly slid into another seat. The poor guy with the exposed ears waited a block or two, then pulled the cord, ran off the bus.

"Yup," said the woman with the fire red hair, "we're turning out a bunch of weak men and strong women. You can't find a man who wants to work these days. I guess it's the woman's turn to run things for the next thousand years."

I was too beat to say anything. I thought back to the days in the sixties when I'd attended elementary school in an all-white suburban school, when I was told how lucky I was to be American, when I knew how lucky I was to be white and male.

I was one of those people who could ride in the front of the bus. And do you know what I thought, back then? I believed I was the only passenger on the planet earth, that I lived on what seemed to be a never-changing schedule, where some great, white, male dispatcher made sure the bus would come for me alone. But that bus never came.

That was how this woman with fire-red hair was thinking now. The whole town and its people were just one big table for her to dance on in the night club of American life. I guess she was trying to say that it was now a woman's turn to drive the bus.

She said, "I've noticed that you people in this town, and I hope nobody takes offense, all seem to walk around with tombstones in your eyes," and that's when I wanted to take her by the hand and show her all the old Movement people I knew who hung around the magazine, burned-out souls, who'd been waiting and waiting for that bus of theirs to come, and now they were about to turn around and go home.

But she pulled the cord and got off at Third and Reily. "Jesus is lord," she said as she got off the bus. As for me, I didn't buy Jesus. I didn't buy women's lib. I didn't buy gay rights or Castro. I was only involved in one movement. The Mass Transit Riders' Movement was the only movement I knew where I could get off anywhere I wanted, and always know just where I was. Uptown. 17th and Market. I'd pull the cord and climb out wherever it suited me. Sometimes I used to think I paid my ninety-five cents in exact change not to get on a mass transit bus, but to get off just where I wanted. I didn't know of any greater bargain.

Nevertheless, I finally got sick of riding the bus. So I broke down and bought Falstaff's car. But after I'd given him the money he wouldn't give me the plate or go to a notary with me to sign the car over. Finally, in a huff of righteous indignation, I stormed over to his house and demanded the damn plate. I could see him watching from behind his curtains as I screwed the license onto the back of the car. I felt bad now about taking his car away from him. Well it wasn't exactly like I'd forced him to sell it to me. I'd gone to great lengths trying to avoid buying it, going as far as Michigan to avoid him. It's not like I had a gun to his head or anything.

One other auspicious thing happened after I got back from my vacation. I moved into Nicholson's house. Nicholson was one of the writers at the magazine. His GI Bill running out, he'd decided to study journalism in Philadelphia before the benefits lapsed. He had a small house within walking distance of the magazine. He'd been living in the house with a woman named Doris, but they'd broken up as the time drew near for him to go away to school.

(Doris, by the way, was a remarkable woman. She liked to tell about how she used to sit on Einstein's lap. When she was a little girl in Philadelphia she'd sometimes go to the home of a friend and find Albert Einstein playing the violin. Einstein had come to visit an old German couple he'd known from his European days. They'd be playing Viennese waltzes. Doris used to tell me about Einstein's unkempt yellow white hair. The shoulders of his rumpled jacket would invariably be speckled like stars with dandruff. When the children came in Einstein would set down his violin. Gathering them up in his lap, he'd draw open a book of Winnie the Pooh stories. Together, on Einstein's lap, they'd get lost in the universe at Pooh Corner.)

Anyway, Nicholson asked me to move in and look after things while he was gone. He only wanted seventy-five dollars a month rent. Part of the deal was that he'd be able to come into town on weekends and whore it up in one of the upstairs bedrooms. In addition to Doris, he'd been seeing a married woman on the side. In return for the low rent, he wanted occasional access to one of the rooms.

His place was a cheery little row house tucked in an alley. It was painted yellow, and always seemed to catch the sun squeezing in through the big craggy old frame houses on Third Street.

I can't tell you how much of a step up in the world it was for me to be living in a house all by myself. I'd shared houses with friends before but I'd never had a place all to myself. The first night I laid on the bare carpet in the living room proudly surveying my castle. Aside from my carpet and my stereo and my bed (I'd put the bed in the sunny, front bedroom) the place was without a stick of furniture. Still, I'd never had a house all to my own before. After a day at the office it felt good to walk the brick sidewalks home.

I hadn't been there more than a couple of days when I got a phone call from Nate Freeman.

"This friend of mine needs of a place to stay," he told me. "She doesn't have much money. I told her maybe you'd rent her a room."

He said he'd bring her by after work. Freeman knew some attractive women. He also knew some dogs. I had no way of knowing that he wouldn't bring over one of the dogs but lately I'd been feeling lucky.

That evening when I pulled up in my new car I found Freeman waiting on the porch with a woman who looked like Sissy Spacek. Do you know the type? Long, straight hair braided down the side of her head. Slim, yet flaring hips. Delicate, yet distinct cheek bones. High forehead.

I'd only seen her once before. She'd been working for the town's feminist newsletter. The feminists rented a small room from the magazine, on the third floor next to our layout room, where they shared some of our layout equipment. The room they rented was actually a bedroom, with a beat-up bed in one corner where our paper's editors used to commit all sorts of transgressions with college interns. The feminists would sometimes be forced to use the bed as a layout table. They resented that their office was a bedroom, but it was the only space we had.

One evening when we were due at the printer the next day I'd come into the layout room and found the feminists using our layout tables. I kicked them all out, in the brusque way of an editor facing a deadline. The women went back to their office next to the layout room to use the bed for paste-up. I could hear them sulking angrily in low tones.

"Men! This is always what happens when you rely on them!"

"Why do they all have to be so damn domineering!"

I hadn't been laying out the magazine for more than a couple of minutes when two dogs — a German shepherd and an Irish setter — came suddenly up the steps and ran into the layout room, eyeing me. Then the woman who looked like Sissy Spacek came up the steps and had gone into the feminist's office, calling the dogs.

Now she was on my front porch, wanting to rent a room.

I parked the car and went up onto the porch. Freeman introduced us.

"This is Sterling North."

We shook hands.

"You'll have to forgive me if I forget your name," I told her. "It always takes me three times to remember a name."

"Well at least you're honest."

I showed her around the house, apologizing for the lack of furniture.

"That's all right," she said. "I've got plenty. I was wondering what I was going to do with it all. If I decide to move in I'll just bring it along."

"Great."

"You say you don't mind dogs?"

"Dogs? I love dogs. I don't mind dogs at all."

"Nate told me you're only paying seventy-five dollars a month."

"That's right."

She had a way of moving her lower jaw.

"That's very reasonable, all right. How much would you charge me for a room?"

"I guess half of that. What's that? Thirty-eight dollars a month?"

She moved her jaw again.

"You mean thirty-seven fifty."

I smiled.

We were standing in the sunny, front bedroom, beside my bed. She pounded the floor with her foot.

"I think this floor will support my waterbed," she said. "I'd like this room."

"This room? Well I was--." I stopped myself.

Later that night I moved my bed out of the sunny, front bedroom, to a smaller, darker room in the back of the house. She moved in the next day. She brought a houseful of furniture and two dogs.

6.

I don't know where she'd come from or what the world had done to drive her to my door. Freeman told me she'd been having trouble with men.

"She's so beautiful that men keep hitting her up for sex," he told me after he'd brought her over and she'd moved in. "It's driving her nuts."

"And you figured I wouldn't hit her up?"

"All you care about is that damn magazine of yours."

"Oh I see. So naturally you thought we'd be perfect together."

"Actually I wanted to move in with her myself but I don't have the nerve. She's safe if she's with you. I thought my bringing her here was a stroke of genius."

Not that I minded. She *was* beautiful. Now when I walked those miserable cracked brick sidewalks home from the office at day's end there'd she'd be, perhaps reading a Balzac novel in a swatch of warm sunlight by a window, or maybe cooking tremendous vegetarian food in the kitchen.

The first evening I came home from work her big dogs barked and bounced around me when I walked in.

"Godwit! Goldeneye! Get down!"

The dogs liked me. I could charm the ass off a dog, if I wanted to. They sat, wagging tails while I patted and stroked them.

"That's unusual. They don't usually take to strangers."

She was in the kitchen, making dinner. I sat on the carpet in the next room, playing records, talking to her through the archway between the two rooms. She'd stuck an "I love Philadelphia" bumper sticker to the refrigerator.

"Do you like Philadelphia?" I asked her.

"I didn't used to. But I think it's come a long way. I enjoy going there now."

"Do you drive or do you take the train?"

"Oh, I drive my truck." She had one of those small imported pickups. "I bought it with the last of the money from my big-paying job. Before I quit."

"Where did you work?"

"At an army depot."

"What did you do there?"

"I ordered parts for weapons. I hated it."

"How'd you get that job?"

"My father. He works for army procurement."

"Where's that?"

"Where I come from. In Wilkes-Barre."

"Really? My family's from Scranton."

"No kidding? Well my father thought I should apply for the job. I hated it."

"Why?"

She made that funny motion with her mouth.

"Other than the stupidity of ordering parts for weapons? Those men over at the depot. They're all the same. And the women too, for that matter."

"I know what you mean. The men spending all their time in search of an orgasm and the women pretending they're not."

She looked at me. "Exactly. I had to get out. Maybe I was afraid I'd end up like them if I didn't get out. I'd saved up some money so I bought the truck and left."

About this time she'd handed me a jar she couldn't open. I gave it a good twist and the lid came off.

"I don't know why I let you open it," she said. She took the olives back into the kitchen. "My feminist friends have a saying: 'The jars always seem to open when there's not a man around.'"

"You're a feminist then?"

"Of course. Aren't you?"

"I haven't given it much thought." I was quiet for a moment, stuck for something to say. "You know, you *could* take the train to Philadelphia."

She laughed.

"I couldn't get down to the train station. Where would I park my truck?"

"That's easy. You can take the city bus down to the station."

"I couldn't do that."

"Why not?"

She was smiling, her eyes all lit up.

"I don't know how to stop the bus."

"You pull the cord."

"That's what I've been told. But I've never ridden one so I don't know."

"You're a funny blend of a feminist. You feel guilty about asking a man to open a jar yet you don't know how to get off a bus."

I made her laugh.

"Look," she said. "I'm making dinner. I'll cook if you clean up."

"Deal."

But I didn't leave it at that. I helped make dinner. She was amazed to find a man who knew his way around the kitchen.

Most of the men she knew, she said as I sliced vegetables for the salad, didn't even know how to hold a knife.

"You don't know the right men, is all," I told her. "Someday you'll make someone a good wife."

After we ate she went up to her room then returned with a psychology textbook.

"In school I was a psych major," she said. She was thumbing through the book. "Here's what I'm looking for, right here."

She folded back the book. Would I like to take a quiz? she asked.

"What kind of quiz?"

"A psychological profile. It's meant to show your sexual orientation. Do you mind?"

"Well I don't know."

"It won't be so bad."

She started asking questions, keeping track of my answers on a yellow pad. If someone was rude would I pick a fight or walk away? If someone was tailgating me on the freeway how would I react? After she'd asked all the questions she totaled it up. She seemed surprised.

"I don't believe it."

"What don't you believe?"

"I've heard about people like you. Until now I've never met one."

"Met one what?"

"You see, if I total your score and you have a positive number, you have a masculine personality. If you score a negative number you'd have feminine personality traits."

"How'd I do?"

"You came out a perfect zero. You're androgynous."

It was about then that Freeman knocked. The three of us played Scrabble until almost eleven. At last Sterling said she was tired and was going to bed. She went up the stairs, called her dogs, which followed her up, then closed the door to her room. I sat quietly wondering whether Freeman would follow her up. He didn't. He stayed talking with me in the living room for about an hour, and put away the Scrabble tiles. Then he left.

7.

Freeman soon left town altogether. For some time his father had been on him to quit traveling and writing and find a real job. His old girlfriend — the one he'd traveled all around the country with in the van — called one day and offered to sell him the van. She was working at a small publishing company in Seattle and offered to sell him the van for a thousand dollars if he'd come to work for the company. She'd deduct the cost of the van from his paycheck. He thought it would be a good way to buy the van and do some traveling so he accepted her offer. His father, overjoyed to be getting Nate out of the house, dropped him off at the train station.

Sterling and I had said good-bye to Freeman the night before, so we were surprised to get a phone call from him on the morning of his departure. He'd forgotten his rail pass, and had to get off the train at the next stop down the line. To avoid reporting to his job he'd bought a two-week rail pass. He planned to travel to Seattle by way of New Orleans, Denver, Salt Lake, Los Angeles and points west. The conductor was coming down the aisle when Freeman realized he'd forgotten the pass. Just then the train made its first stop and he jumped off with his things, the conductors yelling at him as he ran from the tracks.

Now he wanted Sterling to go back to his parents' house and search for his ticket. His parents wouldn't be home all day, he said, but even so he didn't want to risk going there because his father had made such a big deal of dropping him off at the train station and all. Sterling, not wanting to go alone, asked me to come along.

His parents' house was in the suburbs. We let ourselves in with a key they always kept under the mat. I showed Sterling the wonder of the Freemans' house, Nate's bedroom, the walls and ceilings of which were completely covered with articles and photographs he'd cut out from newspapers and magazines over nearly twenty years. His vast book shelves took up much of the space of his room, while his four thousand-album record collection filled three closets.

The Freemans were great collectors. I knew we were going to have trouble finding a mislaid rail pass in the middle of such bric-a-brac. While Sterling scouted around I sat down at the piano and tapped out a melody.

"I feel funny going through someone's house like this," I heard her call out.

She came and stood by the piano.

"What's this?"

She spotted the rail pass lying on top of the upright piano. It was real luck.

We locked the house and drove down to the train stop to pick up Nate. There he was, out in front of the small depot, flying a kite. He seemed pretty unhappy. You could tell he didn't want to take the job in Seattle. I suppose if he could he'd forever be out there flying a kite.

He reluctantly reeled in the string, folded up his kite, and had us take him back to our house. He stayed with Sterling and me for several days, camping in our living room, saying he didn't have to be in Seattle for another two weeks. The whole time he never went outside, so worried was he that he might run into his father somewhere out in the street. I felt sad for him when I dropped him off at the train station at the end of the week. Some era in both our lives was ending, I knew.

8.

I don't know what the world had done to drive her to my door. I'm sure she would tell you I've got it all wrong, that I've forgotten the important parts and exaggerated the parts that don't matter. You can never get the story right to some people's satisfaction. The important thing is that I think she was hiding. Most of the day she'd disappear into her room, she said to write poetry. Maybe she was using her verses to hide from her memories. I didn't mind because I was hiding too, hiding from my own set of disappointments. Needing time out, we both retreated into Nicholson's house to lick our wounds.

She brought with her to the house knickknacks from failed relationships with men I'd never meet. She put the knick-knacks in the front room of the house, where we never sat, so that they were always out of sight. It was kind of a museum to failed relationships. She wouldn't tell me much, only little pieces, and then only late at night when she sat drinking wine with me at the kitchen table, her smile gay and warm, her head in her hand, leaning over the table, her eyes remembering all the men from whom she said she'd "escaped."

There was a rocking chair made by a man she'd known in

college, now somewhere out West. There were gifts from all the men who had chased after her when she'd spent a year touring Europe and the Middle East with her sister. There was a flute given her by a man from Scotland. She laughed, explaining she'd met the Scot at a kibbutz in Israel, of all places. One night he'd tried to break down her door to see her, and yelled through the blocked door in a thick Scottish accent, "Aye wunt tue teach you Scutch!" The men in Europe were rude and ignorant, she said, but she'd liked Israel. "I could have stayed there. But I had my doggies to get back to, didn't I?"

She was stroking her setter. "As it was, I overstayed Israel four months, and the idiots who were watching Goldeneye tied her to a tree and ever since she's had a nervous twitch. Poor Goldeneye."

Also in her museum was a self-portrait of a young man, an artist, who'd lived with her for several years. It was really a hideous painting, I thought, not well drawn, with outrageous colors, but she said she liked it and hung it on the wall of the front room, in a corner where you had to go out of your way to see it. I couldn't get much out of her about the guy who painted it. Like the painting, the back corners of her mind were hard to see.

"We were almost as good as married," she once let slip. "God how I hated that. Being someone's wife. Putting up with all the things no self-respecting human being would ever put up with. The other person starts off wanting you to read the same books he's read. He wants you to think like him, be like him. Before you know it, it's Yes dear this and Yes dear that. Honey this honey that. It makes me want to puke. That's not love. That's-- that's imprisonment."

She laughed.

"You know what? When I was at the market today the woman who sold me bread called me 'Hun.' 'Enjoy the bread, hun.' Why do people say that?"

"You don't believe in marriage then?"

"I don't believe it's good to be totally dependent on any one person. That's what always goes wrong." She made that funny motion with her mouth. "It's unrealistic to imagine one person can supply all your needs."

One afternoon she asked me if I would mind keeping my guitar in the room filled with relics from the men in her past.

"I didn't give it to you yet," I joked, but she didn't get me. She only stood puzzled.

She'd merely wanted to get my guitar case out of the hallway. "I thought the front room was a good place to store it," she said.

9.

In the mornings I'd wake up hearing the door to Sterling's room open. I'd hear the sounds of her dogs vaulting from the room, the sounds of their nails scratching the hardwood floors as they tore down the hall, then the sounds of Sterling's footsteps. Soon I'd smell coffee brewing in the kitchen.

I'd get up and we'd sit and talk over coffee. One morning I walked her dogs with her. We walked the three blocks to the river and let the dogs run loose.

"The river's beautiful here," she said as we walked along. "It's so wide. It's nothing like this in Wilkes-Barre."

"People here take it for granted," I told her. "Sometimes, the way it rolls by, it reminds me of life. Big, central, ignored. Slowly rolling by, unappreciated, like life itself."

We walked along the slow muddy river, the dogs running at our heels, until we came to Verbeke Street. We cut up to the farmers market. It was early in the morning and most of the farmers were still unloading their trucks. We tied the dogs to a pole and went in. Old women sat at their stalls selling sweet rolls and eggs. In the back we found a penny candy stand. A man in a Phillies cap was arranging red licorice in a jar. I bought two sticks and gave one to Sterling.

"You know what I used to like?" she said. We were walking along, eating the licorice. "Wax lips."

"You mean those fake lips made of wax that come in all different colors?"

"Uh-huh. I haven't seen them in ages."

The next morning, a Saturday, I awoke when I heard the door to Sterling's room open. I heard the scratchy sounds of her dogs bolting from the room, followed by her footsteps. Soon there was a pounding on the front door, and I heard the sounds of Sterling letting someone in. Heavy footsteps coming up the stairs. My door flung open. I sat up in bed.

It was John, my biker friend. He came in wearing a leather jacket. A chain from one of those biker wallets hung from his back pocket. He seemed surprised to find me in my bed. He looked down the hall, to Sterling's open door, taking in a corner of her unmade waterbed, a confused expression on his face.

"Mr. Parker, good morning," he said, pacing the floor. "Want to cruise over to the motorcycle shop with me? I need a new choke for my panhead."

I wanted to go shopping anyway. I'd gotten it in my mind to find Sterling some wax lips.

I got out of bed and threw on some clothes. We took John's Harley. I made him stop at every farmers market and candy store along the way. I just had to lay my hands on a pair of wax lips. The two of us walked up to candy counter after candy counter, trying to keep a straight face while I asked for the wax lips. But nobody had any wax lips. Finally, downhearted, I threw in the towel and we went to the motorcycle shop. By coincidence there was a penny candy counter in one corner of the bike shop. John, who by now was into the search, went up to the macho owner of the motorcycle shop and asked, in a low voice, "Would you happen to have wax lips?" He motioned to his mouth.

At first the guy wouldn't answer.

Then, "No. You don't see them no more. They don't make them no more."

Could it be? They didn't make wax lips any more?

I tried to put the whole episode out of my mind, though I couldn't help thinking that something special had gone out of the world. Then about a week later I got a package in the mail. Opening it I was surprised to find bright red, green, blue, and yellow wax lips grinning up at me from the box. John had been motorcycling through the Midwest and had found them in some candy store in Indiana. Later when Sterling came in I stood at the stove with my back to her, wearing a pair of red wax lips while I stirred a pot of soup. She talked about her day but I wouldn't reply. Several times I turned around, shook my head as she spoke. She didn't seem to notice. Then her eyes caught the lips. She came over for a closer look.

"Oh," she said. "I haven't seen those things in years."

Later that evening she asked me, "Do you mind if I have company over?"

"Why should I mind?"

The next night when I came home from work Sterling was seated at the kitchen table with a man. They were making pizza. He was much older than I, in his mid-thirties, at least, and bearded. He seemed rather taken aback when I came in. When I shook his hand he looked at me in an odd way, like he didn't know what to make of me. "This is my new roommate," Sterling told him. He was cutting up mushrooms for the pizza. They invited me to have some with them. He turned out to be an old friend of Sterling's. Not a bad guy. After we ate dinner he left.

The following Saturday morning I heard Sterling giving directions over the phone. She was telling someone how to get to the house from Philadelphia. In the early afternoon we heard a knock. The dogs ran barking to the door. Sterling let in a young man in his mid-twenties, bearded, about my height, but stockier. He greeted her at the door with a kiss and several soft words that I couldn't hear. She brought the guy into the kitchen.

"This is my friend Hank," she told me. "He's a medical student in Philadelphia."

"How do you do?" I said.

We sat down to chat. He said his trip from Philadelphia had only taken him an hour and a half, "Not bad," he said.

I had work to do that afternoon at the office and excused myself. The two of them were going shopping downtown. I said I'd run into them later. When I got back from work that evening they'd just finished dinner and were still at the table. Dinner plates, an empty bottle of wine, and glasses were spread out before them.

"We should have saved you some wine," Hank said.

"That's all right. Maybe I should run and get more though while the liquor store is still open."

"If you want I'll drive you."

We took Hank's car up to the liquor store. It was a beat up little two-seater, a Bradley GT with a loud engine. The ride to the liquor store was a short one. We didn't have much to say to each other. He idled the car out front while I ran in and bought a gallon of cheap red wine.

When we got back to the house the three of us sat talking at the kitchen table. I put on a record and opened the wine. Hank said he didn't want any. He looked at the bottle like it wasn't good enough for him. After I poured myself some I ran for my corncob to get them high.

"You have a nice car," Hank said to me.

"Thanks. I got a good deal from a friend."

"Hank also thinks you have a nice stereo," Sterling said.

"It's a stereo," I said.

"It's a nice amp," Hank said. "Maybe you could use a new stylus though."

"I guess I don't pay too much attention to it. I just like to listen to records."

"You have a nice record collection," Hank said.

"Thanks. I like to listen to records while I work."

"You have a nice typewriter," Hank said. "I saw it when Sterling was showing me around upstairs."

"Thanks. I haven't had much chance to use it lately."

I got up to flip the record. We were listening to Hey Jude.

"This is a nice record," Hank said.

"Yes. I don't think there's a bad song on it."

"There aren't too many other records without a bad song."

"No, not too many others I can think of."

We tried to think of others. Nothing came immediately to mind.

"Tapestry. By Carole King," I offered. "There's only one or two losers on that."

"Tapestry," Sterling said. "Yes, that's a good record."

"Yeah, it's a nice record," Hank agreed.

I got Hank so high that he started talking about medical school.

"I'd have trouble dissecting corpses," I confessed to him.

"It's a little hard at first. But after awhile you get used to it. We even joke around."

"How do you mean?"

"Someone might put a hand or an ear in the pocket of your lab smock. Stuff like that. There's a clown in every class."

"Still they must teach you there's a proper way to treat a corpse."

"Yes, there's a certain decorum with which you're taught to treat the dead."

Me, I thought Hank was dead. I was treating him with a

certain decorum.

    Sterling got up from the table. Stretching, she piled her hair on her head. Goldeneye, her Irish setter, lay close on the floor beside the German shepherd.

    "Goldeneye," Sterling said, and the dog got up and came over. Sterling stroked the setter's red hair. "Was Goldeneye lying down? Yes she was. Yes she was." Godwit came over for his pats. Sterling patted him vigorously on his flat forehead. He seemed to smile. "Yes Goldeneye's so happy. Yes she is. She won't have to sleep alone tonight."

    The conversation petered off. I went into the living room and took my guitar from the case. For some time I sat softly playing the guitar and drinking wine, until Sterling and Hank went up the steps. I heard the door to her room closing.

    Early the next morning, before dawn, I was awakened by the sounds of Hank washing in the bathroom. After awhile I heard the sounds of the front door being closed, and the sounds of Sterling walking alone back up the steps to her room, closing her door. For quite some time I lay awake, watching the gradual morning light give color to the box of wax lips smiling up from the table by my bed.

10.

The next weekend my friend Mike came in from college. He was upset. It turned out John Baines had made good his threat. Once he'd gotten settled in Yellow Springs, Ohio, he'd written his girl, telling her what I'd said about her two-timing with Mike, asking if it was true. Of course she'd denied it. Then she'd straightaway written Mike, telling him all about it. Now Mike was on my doorstep, livid. It was a touchy situation.

I told Mike I hadn't thought Baines would actually write any letters. "Someone could get punched in the nose for something like this," I stammered. Mike stood there looking at me, his shoulders hunched, like he was about to do the honors.

I managed to calm him down.

"Ah, we can't let these women come between us, Michael old boy. How about a beer?"

We drank a beer.

"I think I'm in love," I told him.

"How do you know?"

"I'm doing all kinds of crazy things."

"That's a reliable sign. Anyone I know?"

"No."

"When did you decide this?"

"I've been trying to place the exact moment. I think it must have been when I first met her. Or maybe it was a few minutes later, when I showed her my bedroom."

"You got her into your bedroom a few minutes after you met her?"

"Yes, and then she kicked me out. It's not what you think, Mike. She's my housemate."

"You've fallen in love with your housemate?"

I nodded the sad truth.

"Oh, that's hell."

"I'm not sure what to do."

"Have you told her?"

"No."

"Well that's the first thing you have to do. Then you must do what you must to get her. But you know that."

All the next day Mike went around town with Sterling and me. We went down to Italian Lake. The water was still and smooth. Children were tossing bread to the swans. In the middle of the lake a statue, green with corrosion, basked in the sun. While we walked along I told Sterling the story of the statue. It was of a beautiful local girl whom Hemingway had fallen in love with and who was said to have been his model for the nurse in A Farewell to Arms. She was a flapper who had posed for the statue in the natural, her arms lifted high and her shoulders back, a lithe nymph. The statue created a scandal. It became a white elephant, passed around town from one red-faced donor to the next, until it was hidden away in the small park.

"She must have been beautiful, mustn't she?"

Tall sleepy trees led the way out of the park and down Third Street. We stopped in front of the Catholic church. Its towers looked like the turrets of a castle.

"Let's go in," Mike said.

It was a big church. We passed through the giant doors and stood in the quiet coolness. No one was there.

"Why don't you cross yourself with the holy water?" I said to Mike.

"Why don't you?"

"Not me. Maybe Sterling wants to."

Sterling half smiled. She was taking in the echoing loneliness of the place, stopping to look at the statues. We walked all the way up front to the altar.

"Did you read about the people down in Texas who saw the face of Christ on a taco?" Mike asked, his voice echoing in whispers.

"Was it a taco or an enchilada?"

"I think it was a burrito. Yes, it was the blessed burrito. They saw Christ's face on a burrito and wanted to make it into a shrine. But the church has reservations. They don't want to consecrate a burrito."

"Something like that happened in Wilkes-Barre," Sterling said. "Someone saw the Virgin's face in an altar cloth. It caused a lot of trouble."

"Let's get out of here. I think I see St. Ignatius in the drippings of this candle."

We left the church. I talked them into cutting up to Seventh Street to buy ice so that we could make strawberry ice cream.

Mike and Sterling seemed to hit it off. Around midnight, after Sterling went to bed, Mike said to me "I think I can see what you see in her."

Mike and I had been friends since high school. When he was fourteen or fifteen he'd run away from home with an older girl, hitching across America, and his cross-country exploits made him the legend of tenth grade. He had an intelligent, open face and a very warm and trusting soul. He'd smoke like a fiend, inhaling packs of Kool menthols in a day. He'd spent his childhood in Catholic schools, some of them in pretty rough neighborhoods in the city. He used to tell about how he'd walk to school in the mornings in his parochial school tie and clean white shirt and city kids would jump him. Now that he was grown he always managed to have these great Catholic girlfriends, pure young women who used to say prayers for him.

These days Mike went to college at the University of West Virginia, in Morgantown. That night he somehow managed to talk me into driving him back to school. It was Saturday night and I didn't have anything better to do. At about one in the morning we took off into the night, heading up into the Appalachian hills, talking madly about women. About twenty miles out of Morgantown I smelled something burning. The car suddenly lost power.

"The clutch's burned out!"

There we were, in the middle of dark West Virginia nowhere, at four in the morning.

"Oh! You've got to be careful in West By God Virginia," Mike gasped. "Especially on a dark road at this time of night, and especially longhairs like us. There's some pretty weird people living out here in the sticks."

Ten minutes didn't go by before a pickup stopped, idling in the highway. For a moment I was worried, but the cab light came on and we saw a man and his wife and a couple of kids. They were on their way home from some late night revelry. While the kids looked out the window the man yelled he'd call a wrecker for us as soon as he got home. Twenty minutes later the man came back, this time without his wife and kids. He was a good-hearted man of about forty with a soft Southern drawl. Next thing, here came the wrecker.

"What's the matter heah?" the mechanic asked, hopping down.

"The clutch."

"Say, what kind of car is that?"

"It's an Audi. With front-wheel drive."

"An Audi. We know what that means."

What it meant was an ungodly repair bill. I'd only had the car for a month and already it was broken down in the middle of West By God Virginia. The car was towed. The guy in the pickup offered to drive us to his house, where he said he had a bottle of Black Velvet whisky in his freezer. We could think over our options from there. He had a heart of gold. He liked to hunt, he told us as we drove off, and we could tell this was so by the gun rack in his truck.

When we got to his house everything was dark and quiet. It was a small Appalachian hovel, with gun racks and game pelts everywhere. There were some pictures on the wall of beautiful teenage daughters. Straightaway he went to his freezer and pulled out the Velvet. We took turns doing thick cool shots.

"Now, boys, if you want," he said, his drawl soft, "I'll drive you into Morgantown tonight. Or if you'd rather, you can spend the night here and go to church with us in the morning. Whatever you boys want, that's what I'll do."

The pictures of his daughters made his offer appealing but we were anxious to get on the road and told him so. Without batting an eye he loaded us into his truck and drove us the last twenty miles into Morgantown. By this time it was after five in the morning. I was already dozing off when we got there. The steep hills of the little town seemed like a dream. The stranger dropped us off at Mike's dorm and wouldn't take a cent for gas. The best people in the world live in poor backward West Virginia.

I had to hitch home. In the morning Mike dropped me off at the highway and wished me luck, apologizing awkwardly for the inconvenience. I was about to get one of the best rides of my life. I walked down to the highway and stood beneath the underpass. I hadn't been standing there twenty minutes when here came this pretty girl in a compact car. I put out my thumb but of course she breezed right past. Then I heard a bang. Her muffler had fallen off! She got out, came around to the back of her car and stood there with her head in her hands. I walked over, unhurried.

"Looks like your muffler fell off."

Actually it had only half fallen off but was scraping the ground.

"Oh whatever will I do!" she said. She was just too sweet and delicate to get her hands dirty.

"Do you have a coat hanger?"

She dug around in her car and came up with a wire hanger. In a flash I'd strung the muffler off the ground. We stood there looking at each other.

"Oh," she said, "you were hitchhiking, weren't you? Would you like a ride?"

I hopped in. We introduced each other. She was a student on her way home to Annapolis. The whole time she kept saying she'd never picked up a hitchhiker before in her life, that her parents would die if they found out. She kept saying her boyfriend was captain of the West Virginia football team. After an hour or so she dropped me off at Interstate 81. From there I caught one more ride, this time from a quiet insurance salesman, and I was home in record time.

The clutch cost almost four hundred dollars. The next Saturday I got the money out of the bank and rode the bus to Morgantown. The bus came down from Pittsburgh, making endless local stops, and I tried to pass time by reading a Saul Bellow novel. When I got to Morgantown Mike was nowhere around. I had to hitch almost thirty miles out to the garage.

My first ride was with a crazed biker in a beat-up Mustang. He offered me a can of beer when I got in, which I accepted. His hair was long and stringy and he was missing two front teeth. Two tattoos on his arms read, "Live to ride," and "I love my Harley." He had the chassis number of his motorcycle tattooed on his other arm. I was worried about the four hundred dollars bulging in my pocket. Looking for something to say to ingratiate myself I pointed to a tattoo.

"Ah, I see you're a Harley man."

That set him off on a wild patter about his bike and how much he loved it. He said he was on his way to a biker's outing and asked if I'd like to come along. I turned him down, saying I had to get my car out of the garage before it closed for the weekend. When we reached the exit where he had to turn off he let me out with a wave and a handshake. After standing in the desolate highway for about ten minutes two somber mountain men in a pickup pulled over. They had a meanness in their eyes. The whole trip neither said a word.

I sat between them in the front seat of the pickup, the whole time expecting the worst, and I breathed a sigh of relief when they finally dropped me off at my exit. I walked over a hill to the garage. My car sat out front. The mechanic seemed surprised to see me. He said he hadn't expected me till Monday.

"Isn't it done?"

"Oh yeah, hmm hmm, it's done all right," he said.

He seemed uneasy, and I couldn't figure it out. He led me out to my car and removed two fishing rods and a tackle box from the backseat. He hadn't been expecting me till after the weekend and was about to take my car on a fishing expedition.

11.

The next day, a Sunday, Sterling and I went to an art show at the museum. It felt good to walk beside her, to be seen with her. We saw a dance troupe perform in the auditorium.
 "They're not too good," Sterling whispered about the dancers.
 "How can you tell?"
 "I just know. If you'd ever seen a good dance troupe you'd know what I mean."
 Afterwards we looked at the paintings. Wordlessly we walked into an auditorium and sat in front row seats to watch a musical group perform. When we left the museum Sterling started running across the street. I ran after her and caught up, running beside her.
 "You can't outrun me," I told her.
 She strained to get away, but I held on, until at last she seemed to resign herself.
 That evening, after dinner, we sat at the table talking. She told me about some of the women we'd seen that day at the art show. As she spoke she held her wine glass out in front of her, her elbows on the table, her eyes seeming to shine.

"The one woman I introduced you to — the attractive one in the judges' booth — do you know the one I mean? She's just getting over this really neat guy. He wanted to get serious. 'Can't we just be friends?' she asked him. Do you know what he told her? 'I don't like your taste in friends.' Would you believe that?"

She laughed. She moved her mouth in that funny way of hers. Her eyes were shining.

"Why do all the men you know have beards?" I asked.

"What?"

"The men you know. Nate Freeman. Hank. Even the guy you made pizza with the other night. They all have beards."

"Why you're right. That's funny. I never realized it before."

She moved her mouth in that funny way.

"You seem to like the same kind of guys," I told her.

She shrugged.

"Well I certainly don't think you're like any other man I've ever met."

"It's my mystique. I know how to cook."

"You do come with your share of surprises."

"Your friend you had over the other night to make pizza knew how to cook."

"Ken? No, he doesn't cook. I was surprised he even helped by slicing mushrooms that night. Now Hank, he can cook. When we first met we made this big dinner, backwards. We had dessert first and worked our way up to soup, salad, then appetizers."

"Still you seem to like the same sort of guy. That's just my observation."

"Nate Freeman isn't anything like Hank or Ken."

"Don't kid yourself."

"No he's not. One morning I got this note from him. I was staying in a mobile home. I got up and found such a beautiful note from him it endeared me to him forever."

She ran up to her room and got the note. Unfolding it, she held it out to me. It was the same note I'd seen Nate drop off on our way to our trip in Michigan. So now I knew who he'd given it to, but I didn't want to read it.

"I better not."

"Why not?"

"It's not good to read someone else's love notes. Especially a friend's."

"What? Be serious! It's not a love note." She was smiling, a hand on her hip. "Go on, read it."

She kept holding Freeman's note out to me. I took it. Not feeling too good about things I read it. It said that he thought she was beautiful.

I quickly gave it back.

"Of course it's a love note. Are you blind?"

She folded it up, putting it in her shirt pocket. Her hair was done in two braids on either side of her head.

"I remember how special I felt when I got up that morning and read those words," she said. She made that funny motion with her mouth, trying to convey something for which she could find no words. "He's not like any other man I've ever met. He's not trying to take possession of me."

She sat down again at the table, across from me.

"Has any man ever asked you to marry?"

"Yes," she laughed, shaking her head.

"I bet you let them down easy, didn't you?"

She laughed harder still, squirming in her seat.

"Did any of them ever get down on their knees and propose?"

She was cracking up.

"Yes. Now stop. It's not nice to laugh about this."

"Because he doesn't get down on his knees you think Nate Freeman's different from the others, don't you? Well he's just like the others. He's playing his cards better, that's all."

She took my hand, caressing it. Her eyes were shining.
"Promise me you won't end up like the others," she said. She brought her hand over and rubbed my cheek.

12.

About this time, much to my surprise, I finally was named editor of the magazine. An unusual series of events led to my promotion. In the same issue Lenny Popadopolis, the spontaneous human combustion expert, wrote about the hypothetical meltdown at the local nuke, I'd asked Dave Crispen, our accountant-cum-editor, to write an article explaining how the magazine had landed the fifty thousand dollar grant from the federal government. I thought it interesting that a publication that started out as an underground rag in the anti-war days was now receiving Uncle Sam's largesse.

These decisions had a fateful outcome. The electric utility executives were outraged by Lenny Popadopolis' meltdown prediction. Turning a few pages they read Dave Crispen's article, "Feds fund radical rag." The president of the electric utility fired off an angry letter to his congressman, saying our meltdown prediction was outrageous. A meltdown could never happen at *his* nuke. He expressed horror, shock and resentment that a magazine like ours would on top of everything be receiving federal funds. The congressman, himself funded every election by the utility, immediately ordered an investigation of our grant. The next day we got a phone call from the feds saying our funding had been mysteriously terminated.

Dave Crispen resigned on the spot. He'd never understood how the magazine published all those years. He'd seen the federal grant as our only hope for solvency.

"Well I guess this is it," he laughed. "I'm resigning effective immediately."

He said he was going to move to have the magazine declared insolvent.

"You can't do that."

"Why not?"

I told him over the years editors had come and gone, always assuming the duties enthusiastically, then burning out in the small-town gloom. Editors were free to go, I pointed out, but the unwritten rule was that they couldn't shut down the magazine if others wanted to continue.

"But how will you go on?"

I shrugged my shoulders. We'd hired three people whose salaries were paid by the federal grant. The first, an old sixties holdover named Sam, had a bad back and was supposed to be our community reporter. His back unfortunately prevented him from leaving his desk and touring the community. Sam was an interesting person. He kept an incredibly junked-up apartment in a poor section of town. We'd sometimes go there and smoke bongs. He had handmade skull and bones signs pasted to his windows, warning potential intruders in Spanish that the place was protected by invisible death rays. He had great sixties memorabilia that he would show when you came over. The rare Beatles' slaughtered baby album cover. R. Crumb and Fabulous Furry Freak Brothers comics. He also had an almost complete collection of Zippy the Pinhead comics. He liked to tell about the time, when he worked for a beer distributor, he'd brought a case of beer to a home and a pinhead had answered the door, paid wordlessly then carried the beer inside on his shoulder. He even knew the medical name for pinheadedness.

Sam was well-educated and well-read. He had a degree in literature. Because of his bad back — a birth defect — he'd never really applied his degree. We'd spend lots of time talking about all the characters who cough up blood in Dostoevski novels, then the conversation might slip into the beatings or the unspeakable sexual atrocities in Shakespeare and Chaucer. "Thoreau! Egad! His sister used to every day bring his mother's cooking to the cabin!" If he got really souped up he'd commit the ultimate unthinkable heretical offense of his generation and call Kerouac a phony. "Ah, he mostly just rode around on Greyhound buses," he'd say, goggle-eyed, with a dismissive wave. He was always on the lookout for phonies. Sam was really a good, happy fellow, with a bushy moustache and a slumped posture. He had incredible stories of men lost in heroin, women, or war. He never married, though he said he once came close before coming to his senses. He was pals with a short and stubby unemployed silo inspector named Max, who always wore Hawaiian shirts. Max, with no silage to inspect, always ghosted around the office or Sam's apartment.

The second federally funded employee was a loose-jointed, hip black street artist named Eric. Eric would stand around the office all day talking about get rich quick schemes and the conspiracy of the moneyed elite that kept him down.

The third federally funded employee was a welfare case named Laurie, hardly ever around, who we were supposed to be training as a typesetter. She had at least five aliases — Laurie Brown, Laurie Black, Laurie Gray, Laurie White, and Elmira Jefferson. Sometimes we'd get calls for one of these people and we'd take a message.

When they heard our funding had been cut Eric and Laurie left immediately.

"Don't that just jive with the world," Eric said. Cursing his continual bad luck, he walked loose-jointed out the door.

"Well I guess that about finishes that," Laurie said, coming in one day for her final check, her boyfriend idling their car at the curb.

Sam stayed around for a few weeks, until he had to take a temporary job to make rent.

At least we still had our original core of wacky volunteers and board members. There were also a few serious young writers floating around town who could always be cajoled into writing a passable article for nothing. I stuck around purely for career reasons. At last, I figured, I'll be made editor.

It almost didn't go that way. A segment of the board, led by that shrew and priest killer Nancy Downs, said I was too young to edit the rag. I was forced to get tough with various board members. I buttonholed a few of the swing votes, telling them they were bullying me and they knew it, that I deserved the editorship, that I'd been running the magazine for a year now in everything but title and now I deserved that. Anything of any value I've ever wanted I've had to fight for. I don't know how things are in your corner of the world but I've had to fight for everything.

The night of the important board meeting they asked me to leave the room while they talked things over. After a few minutes they called me back in. It was quiet for a moment, then they congratulated me.

After the meeting one of the board members told me I'd gotten the job because the editorship required someone with a heart, "And you don't have one." It was the old hire the handicapped policy.

The evening I was named editor I came home and threw myself with much satisfaction on the sofa. Sterling came out from the kitchen and kissed me on my cheek.

Now that I was boss I did the only thing that made any sense. I took the week off.

The next day I dragged Sterling and her dogs off on a long hike into the woods. I took them up into the mountains where I used to go camping as a boy. It was in late December and the world was frozen over. We walked through a labyrinth of wooded paths. Snow covered the ground and the paths were slippery. Icicles hung down from the trees and the springs were frozen over. The dogs ran ahead while Sterling and I, to keep from falling over, walked hand-in-hand over the slippery ice.

"If I fell would you catch me?" She asked it softly, taking cautious steps over the ice.

"Uh-huh. And you? If I fell would you catch me?"

"Uh-huh."

She stopped and pulled her mitten off with her teeth. She wiped at her nose with the back of her hand, then pulled the mitten back on. Her cheeks were red. She put her arm back through mine.

"Do you ski?" she asked.

"I tried once when I was a boy. I went out with the Cub Scouts. It was a day of living horror. Something like three cub scouts broke their legs. I almost skied through the lodge window. I prefer to ice skate."

"Well I like to ski."

"Downhill or cross-country?"

"Both. You know what else? I'd like to go ice camping. Did you ever go camping in the winter?"

"Sure. It's the best time to go."

"You'll have to take me sometime."

The dogs ran everywhichway through the snow. They spiraled between the trees, steam pouring from their mouths. We made our way over a wooded path, crunching through the snow, until we came to an abandoned cabin. The snow and the icicles made it look like a gingerbread house. The world was frozen over and I felt fine.

We explored around the cabin, built of logs and stone by a

man who'd long since died. Before he died he'd nailed a sign to the side of the cabin calling it Paradise. "This is Paradise," the sign read. "Please don't destroy my cabin." I showed Sterling the sign. I told her how once, back in high school, I'd made the mistake of bringing some acquaintances to the cabin and they'd kicked out a wall and knocked down the stone masonry chimney because it was nice. From that I learned there are some people you can't trust beauty with — they'll only destroy it just because it's beautiful.

When I'd first discovered the cabin there was a lovely summer kitchen, screened in and all, complete with a stove and cooking utensils. "Use this cabin," a sign inside the kitchen had read. "Please take care of my Paradise." When I'd first discovered the cabin there were simple wicker chairs and two cots. Now the wall had been knocked down, the beautiful stone chimney had been destroyed, the furniture had been carted off or kicked in, and the sign that read "Please take care of my Paradise" lay broken in the dirt. Maybe it was my fault for bringing people up there. Or maybe it was the old man's fault for calling the place Paradise.

On one side of the cabin there was a spring. When we broke through the ice we drank the clearest, coldest water you'd ever want to taste. I wanted to take her up to the top of the mountain and show her the grave of a slave who'd been buried there two centuries before. But Sterling didn't want to go. Goldeneye, the Irish setter, was beginning to get snow and ice wedged in her shaggy feet. Sterling wanted to get her out of the cold.

"I can build a fire."

"You wouldn't get it started."

"Sure I would. I'm good at it."

"No. We should go back."

She wanted to go. We started back through the woods and went home.

The day after we'd gone to the decimated cabin I took Sterling to a mountain spring to fetch home some water. Along abandoned railroad tracks and twisting paths we crunched through the snow, this time not holding hands but keeping our distance from each other, taking separate paths, seeing each other only in glimpses as we came out from behind trees into clearings.

After filling our jugs with water we walked back together through the paths to the truck. It was a sparkling cold day and the heater in her truck made you feel all warm and cheery. We had to drive cautiously down the icy mountain roads. Sterling played a jazz tape. Coming down out of the mountains, the edge of the road all sugared with salt, we came upon a health food store at the edge of a small village. Sterling backed the truck into a space and we went in. She was dressed in a blue parka with a big hood. When she came in out of the cold she'd throw off her hood and her face would take you by surprise. It was striking and delicate sitting atop the great bulk of the down parka. I watched her as she made her way around the health food store, picking through the giant bins of grains and flours.

Afterwards we stopped at a coffee, tea, and spice shop down the street. The woman who owned the shop couldn't stop offering us whiffs of teas and pungent coffees. She stood behind the counter in her apron exhorting us, "Here, smell this. You won't *believe* how nice it is!" We bought at least six different kinds of teas — camomile, red zinger ("I don't know if you'll like that," Sterling said, "as it's got *lots* of caffeine."), Earl Grey and others I'd never seen before — and as many different kinds of coffees. That night we built a big fire in the wood-burning stove and bundled the house up tight to keep out the winter. We made a great dinner and sat at the table until very late, laughing over wine. Hands across the table. We had nothing to talk about but ourselves.

My earliest memories, I told her, were of women's breasts.

"As a baby, you see, I was always held by women, and I was always looking at their breasts. Not their naked breasts, as I never saw those. The breasts of the women I knew back then were always hidden behind brassieres and stiff dresses."

"This is very revealing and Freudian," she coughed.

"For the longest time I didn't know women had two breasts," I went on. "The fashions in those days made it look like, how can I say?, a single cantilevered ledge across the chest of a woman, like a book shelf."

I was cracking her up.

"My elementary school principal was a great fan of Dwight Eisenhower," I told her. "One day in fifth grade the principal's voice came over the school intercom, saying, 'Boys and girls, a very great man has died, General Eisenhower.' None of us knew who he was."

"They never much liked Eisenhower in Wilkes-Barre," Sterling said. "Once, when he was sick in the hospital, they ran this outrageous headline in the paper, 'Ike's bowels move!'"

"When did you quit going to church?" I asked her.

"I don't know. In my early teens, I guess."

"Was it hard on your parents?"

"Are you kidding? It was almost as bad as when I became a vegetarian."

"They didn't like it when you quit eating meat?"

"No. Not at all. To this day when I visit them I have to eat meat. It upsets everybody so much I just give in."

"Do you want to know about the last mass I attended as a boy?"

"Sure."

"You know the blessings they offer? The priest, singing in deep baritone, leads the congregation in prayers for lost and suffering souls?"

"Uh-huh."

"Well, one Sunday, at the end of his blessings, the priest — he was an old-time Irish priest with a big red alcoholic's nose — the priest sang, 'And let us pray for our boys who are fighting for us in Northern Ireland,' and the congregation answered back, 'Hear us O Lord!'"

"You're kidding."

"No I'm not. It was about the same time I was finding out about sex. The school's retired football coach, a hallowed man, was called out of retirement to make The Big Speech in health class one day. With much ceremony the class was turned over to him. The old guy stood smiling before us with his hands in his pockets. Then he said, 'Boys, keep your dinkus in your pants and you won't have any trouble.' That was all he said. That was the whole lecture. Then he turned and left the room."

"When I was a child," Sterling said wistfully, "my father used to take me and my sister for popsicles."

"Were you a happy child?"

"No. I thought I was fat and ugly."

"An ugly duckling, huh?"

She smiled, sipping some wine. She certainly looked lovely now.

"I guess every kid worries about being popular."

"Popularity's new for me," she laughed. "Then again, I don't think I was ever very popular. I have my friends. But there's always been something about me that puts off some people. When I was in a New Orleans bar two years ago for Mardi Gras someone stepped out of the crowd and hit me in the face."

"Who?"

"I don't know who she was. Some wild-looking woman. She just stepped right up and slugged me in the face."

"Why?"

"I'm telling you, she was a total stranger."

"I used to worry all the time about getting beat up. I used

to study karate. When I was young I used to watch Kung Fu on TV."

She laughed, "I think I'll call you Grasshopper."

The next day I wrote her a note, saying her heart to me was like a pebble, and I now realized when I was quick and strong and clever enough to snatch it away from her it would be time for me to leave.

I don't know where she'd come from or what the world had done to drive her to my door. Late at night, at the kitchen table, I'd continue my investigations, picking up occasional clues.

Beneath her blue eyes, her long brown hair, her slender profile, her studied coolness, there was a darker side, hidden away and burning with scorching intensity in the coolness. One night, holding my hand across the table, she said to me, "Grasshopper, you should have known me when I was younger. You would have liked me so much more. I was happier then."

I got her a job typesetting with a printer downtown. Marvelous work, typesetting. Twenty dollars an hour. My security blanket. The fallback of American writers from Franklin and Twain on down. If you won't let me tell you about your heart at least I'll set your ad copy. I'll sell your wares, your old lawn mowers, your living room suite that you must sell following the unexplained and unexpected breakup of your marriage. One day a friend of mine saw Sterling on her way home from work. He told me, "There's something troubling her. You can see it in her face. I would have stopped her to say hello but the thing in her face scared me off."

A few nights later I was sitting with Sterling at the kitchen table, peeling vegetables, when she said, "I don't know whether I can trust you not to bring me pain." She looked down to a paring knife on the table. "How do I know if you had that knife you wouldn't cut me?" She brought her finger down across her palm, as if cutting it with a knife.

Later that night she came down from her room with a psychology magazine.

"There's a good article in here about incubus and succubus," she said, making tea.

"Incubus and succubus? What're they?"

"It's like a night terror. Incubus is Latin for 'to lie upon.' In the middle ages people believed devillike evil spirits came into their rooms at night and had intercourse with them. This article explains the psychological manifestations of the terror."

"What happens?"

"The incubus has sex with the victim. Or so the victim believed. Perhaps it was just a dream representation of suppressed sexuality. Or maybe, because people believed in the actual physical existence of the incubus, the episodes were concocted to account for illicit pregnancies. An abortion then could be easily sanctioned, since it was believed the woman was carrying a child by the devil. Throughout the ages sex has been equated with black magic, you know. Some of the New England witch burnings can be attributed to women who simply didn't want to have sex with one of the town fathers. The man would say he'd been bewitched by the woman, who'd soon find her days numbered."

"Back to the incubus. What was an encounter with one supposed to be like?"

Sterling was very matter of fact.

"The victim would wake feeling a presence in the room. A terrible evil presence. The victim at first would not cry out, uncertain, until the incubus would suddenly show itself. A terrible figure with horns and pointed tail. By which time it's too late to yell. The victim freezes up, as if paralyzed, until she can no longer breathe or cry out. We know today there's a psychological reason for the attack. Mounting terror can actually paralyze. It's an automatic survival strategy, like amnesia, when pain grows to the point where you can only survive by forgetting. Confronted by an incubus, the victim doesn't move."

She froze. I felt unexplainable fright. Half-suppressed terrors of my childhood came rushing back, dreams where I felt a presence of evil, a presence of malevolence moving through the darkness of my sleep. For a moment I too froze.

"Only women were victims?" I finally asked.

"Men were usually visited by succubus, which means 'to lie under.'"

There was a darkness about Sterling that could frighten me no end. This dark, hidden side I wanted to explore, but she would never allow me, or any man, or maybe anyone, I suppose, to get too close to it.

One cold morning the oil furnace broke. I was preoccupied, on my way to work. I absentmindedly said we'd have to call a repairman. She went off the deep end, saying I didn't care, that she was the one who worried about the house. She got me so worked up I had a repairman there within the hour. When I got home later that day she came down the staircase in her bathrobe. She stood a few steps up. She'd been sleeping.

"Grasshopper, I had a dream about you."

"What was it?"

"I dreamed you came home and your hands were dirty. But you brought me a rainbow."

She came down off the steps, kissed me on the lips. I could feel the dark part of her burning somewhere inside, just out of reach, as real as that incubus in the night. Incubus come to take my love. Then she turned and went back up the steps.

Winter now was in full swing. One evening a friend of Sterling's from feminist circles, Patty, came over for dinner. Patty had a bubbly personality and curly brown hair. She'd recently separated from her husband.

Patty spoke favorably with Sterling about a new periodical, Sphere Magazine, which she said contained the latest articles on crimes against women such as rape and abandonment, and the general male conspiracy.

"Fear Magazine?" I asked.

"No," she laughed. "*Sphere* Magazine."

We spent most of dinner talking about Nate Freeman. It turned out Patty had known Freeman for years, and in fact had been the one who introduced him to Sterling.

"I keep having bizarre contacts with Freeman," Patty said. She explained that she and her estranged husband, before they separated, had decided to take a last-ditch trip to the Virginia wilderness to see if their marriage could be saved. They were out in the woods, in the middle of nowhere, when, by the most remarkable coincidence, who should walk down the path but Nate Freeman. Freeman had been driving up from Florida and by chance had stopped at the same park where Patty and her husband were camped. Patty's husband was a big, jealous weight-lifter.

Freeman didn't feel too welcome. A few months later, before Freeman left for his job in Seattle, Patty asked him over for dinner. Her husband had moved out a few weeks before. She and Freeman were enjoying a quiet meal when suddenly her jealous estranged husband showed up and started pounding on the door. He yelled he saw Freeman in there. Remembering the bizarre encounter in the woods, he became incensed, yelling loud enough for the whole neighborhood to hear that he wasn't a fool, that he knew she'd been having an affair with Freeman. It was a bad scene and for a few minutes things hadn't looked too good for Freeman. Patty had had to threaten to call the police before her husband would go.

After dinner we drank wine and played one record after another. Sterling and I had taken to communicating by stereo. I played a Van Morrison record. Sterling, remembering some happy memory, sighed, "Van the Man."

"Switch on your electric light
Then we can get down to what is really wrong
I long just to hold you tight
So I can feel you
Sweet lady of the night
I shall reveal you
If you will turn it up, turn it up, a little bit higher, your radio"

I turned up the stereo, a little bit higher, as the record instructed, and Patty laughed. Afterward we danced and sang along with Todd Rundgren: "Love is infectious, I was a victim."

"Once," Patty laughed, "when I was in my early twenties, I was invited to a party and, stepping inside, I found myself in the middle of an orgy. People were fucking in the living room."

"Didn't you know what kind of party it was going to be?"

Laughing hysterically, she shook her head no.

"I don't think I've ever told anybody about this before."

"What did you do?"

"Well there was a room, I think the kitchen, where people weren't fucking. A bunch of us congregated there. We tried to act nonchalant about this orgy that was going on around us. I didn't stay very long."

"I once had a bizarre experience at a party," Sterling threw in, "though not quite as bizarre as that. I showed up for the party and this guy had a Veg-O-Matic on his fireplace mantel. You know, one of those things that slices and dices? He had it on his fireplace mantel, in a place of honor."

"What did he do with it?"

"I don't know. I didn't stick around to find out."

I put on a bluegrass record. Sterling, her eyes dreamy, said she knew of this great bar out in the country where people danced and there was always good bluegrass.

"A peanut bar," she said. "You know, one of those places with peanut shells all over the floor."

"Why don't we go there?"

"Now? Tonight?"

"Why not?"

"It's really out in the country. It's snowing so hard. Maybe some other time."

"Why don't we just walk down to the Open Hearth then?"

"That sounds like fun," Patty said. "Mind if I come along?"

"You are kind of horning in on my date with Ms. North," I told her.

"If I go I'll have to spend the night here. On the sofa."

"You can sleep with me on my bed," Sterling told her.

"All right then."

The three of us bundled up and went out into the snowy streets. It was coming down in fine flakes. The snow made the dirty city streets seem clean and new. Not a soul was stirring. We took all the back alleys, walking like stiff moonmen in our winter coats, throwing snowballs, laughing.

"You know," Patty said, steam rising from her cherry mouth as we walked along, "this is a pretty rough part of town. Normally I'd never walk down these alleys at midnight. The snow makes everything so pure, doesn't it?"

"Tom makes us feel safe," Sterling said. I took her by the arm and we walked along.

The bar was a good ten blocks but the snow made the walk enjoyable. For a weeknight the place was hopping. Falstaff and our reporter friend Jenkins had a table by the roaring fire. "Ah, Parker, have a seat," Jenkins called out. He was looking at the women. I introduced them. We had several beers. The whole time Jenkins and Falstaff tried to put moves on Patty and Sterling. They of course got nowhere. Afterward, as we walked home through the falling snow, Sterling and Patty had a good laugh over it.

A few days before Christmas we put up a little tree. Sterling found the tree in a snowy lot in the city. I think she paid the tree farmer five bucks. We made a big deal about decorating it. We strung it with paper chains and popcorn, colored balls and white blinking lights. An angel on the top blew a horn. Sterling threw the left-over popcorn to the barking dogs, one piece at a time. They'd jump in the air and nab it.

Mike showed up on Christmas break. With him he brought a cute young woman with straight strawberry blonde hair. Her name was Kate. She was a very proper Catholic girl. They'd met in school. I gave them some ice cream and some fresh bread. Kate was a lovely girl. We had a nice little party in the kitchen, drinking beer and wine and making drunken toasts to each other. After it was over, on her way out the door, Kate insisted I give her my recipes.

A few days before Christmas Sterling and I stopped by the office to see if there were any messages. While I was going through my mail our newly unemployed typesetter, Laurie, came in. She said she was having trouble getting back on welfare. The welfare bureaucrats were giving her a hard time because she'd received training money from the magazine. Making matters worse, there was a waiting period before she could receive any unemployment comp. Here it was a few days before Christmas and she had no money for presents for her children.

"Those fuckers," I spat.

Sterling leaned in the doorway, listening to Laurie's story.

"I have some money," she told Laurie. "You can borrow a couple hundred. Pay me back when you can."

Laurie didn't brighten.

"No, I couldn't borrow money from you."

Before long Laurie got up and padded downhearted from the

office.

"You shouldn't have offered her money in front of everyone," I said to Sterling. "Didn't you see how much she was embarrassed?"

"I figured since she was talking about it--."

"Well she wasn't asking for a handout. She was talking about how fucked up the bureaucrats are."

Sterling said nothing. I thought that was the end of it. A few years later, after I'd left the magazine, I ran into Laurie on the street.

"What a good person that Sterling North was," she told me. "You know she came by my house the day before Christmas eve and gave me two hundred dollars?"

That wasn't all. It turned out Sterling had her friend Ken, whom I met the night they were making pizza, dress up as Santa Claus and deliver a bag of toys to Laurie's kids on Christmas eve.

"Here I was sure it was going to be such a bleak Christmas," Laurie laughed. "Then we hear a knock on the door. A stranger came in dressed as Santie Claus, with a bag of toys. If you could have seen the looks on the faces of those kids as they hung all over their Santie Claus."

Laurie had been sure Santa Claus had the wrong address and was handing out toys to the wrong kids. As he was about to leave, to convince her not to worry, Ken whispered to Laurie that Sterling had put him up to it.

"That Sterling North has a heart of gold," Laurie told me years later.

Over Christmas Sterling went home to Wilkes-Barre to see her folks. I saw her off at the door. I took her scarf from the hook on the wall and wrapped it tight around her neck.

"Take care out there. It's a cold world."

When she got back after the holiday she had a two-man tent

with her. She laid the tent by the front door, saying she wanted me to take her ice camping.

The next day was New Year's Eve.

"It's customary where I come from," Sterling said, "to cut one's hair on New Year's Eve. It's also a great sign of trust to have someone cut your hair. Would you cut mine?" She held out a pair of scissors.

We laid newspapers down in the kitchen. She sat straight and stiff in the chair. I combed out her silky brown hair. I cut off just the ends. Fine little brown curlicues floated down to the paper.

"Now let me cut yours."

"What?"

She grabbed for the scissors.

"What's the matter? Don't you trust me?"

"No way in hell."

"Come on. Be a sport. Just the ends."

"All right. But just the ends."

I took my place in the chair, hunching my brow as she snipped her way around.

"Your face doesn't look like it trusts me."

Sterling and I discovered that neither of us liked New Year's Eve parties. On the spur of the moment, shortly before midnight, we went down to the railroad terminal to watch the people who didn't have any better place to be. Broken men in sad coats slumped in the benches. We walked around the terminal quietly taking in the sadness of the place.

13.

When I finally got back to work amazing news waited. Our attorney had discovered the electric utility's interference with our funding. He'd filed a complaint and our grant had been restored. Sam, Eric and Laurie came back the next day.

"Don't that just jive with the world," Eric said, walking through the door.

That afternoon I sat at one of the old Remingtons in the office typing out the story of how the electric utility almost shut us down. I called the president of the utility and asked why he'd done it. He snapped there'd never be a meltdown at *his* atomic power plant. "The nuclear industry needs help," he fumed, "not ridiculous panic stories." He spoke over one of those desk intercoms, his voice sounding distant, almost mechanical. "Nuclear's going to go forward," he told me.

Dave Crispen came into the office one day and asked if he could get his editor's job back. I said it was too late. He'd resigned, and now I was editor. But Dave had a big heart, and he continued working around the magazine, keeping the books and writing articles.

Not long after Sterling got back from her holiday she received a call from her sister. I was upstairs typing but overheard. She sounded unhappy.
"Valery! How did that happen?"
There was a pause.
"Well it sounds pretty stupid to me."
Another pause.
"Well of course that's what you should do. The best place to go is Philadelphia. I have a friend you can stay with."
Sterling hung up the phone. She dialed a long distance number.
I heard her say, "Hi, this is Sterling. How are you? Listen, can my little sister stay with you for a day or two?"

About this time my car developed a radiator leak. I went out one morning and tried to fix it. It was a cold morning and I laid on my back in the street beneath the front of the car. Sterling came out to hand tools down to me. The cold made my hands too stiff to work. I laid under the car looking up through the engine at Sterling.

Somehow I managed to patch the leak and a few days later Sterling drove with me to Philadelphia. She'd talked me into running a review of a feminist singer. I arranged free press passes. Outside the concert hall we met up with one of Sterling's friends, a beautiful young woman named Angelica who had long wavy hair. Angelica seemed surprised that I'd come to see the feminist singer.

"Most of the men I know steer clear of feminist events," she told me.

"I thought it might be fun," I said.

We went inside. A big woman was taking tickets. I asked if we could interview the feminist singer. She gave me a look like I was Jack the Ripper. I politely persisted, but it only aggravated her more. She said pushy males never got interviews. I'd embarrassed Sterling and Angelica. They stood on the other side of the lobby pretending they didn't know me. I gave up on the interview and we followed the crowd into the auditorium. The house was jammed. We found our seats and presently the feminist singer came out in a karate uniform. She launched into a song about how it was time for women to start kicking butt, to fight back and beat the crap out of any man who got in her way. As she sang the singer performed karate kicks and punches. Most of the women in the auditorium stood and did the same, singing "Fight back!" I quickly became aware I was the only man in attendance. There I was, smack in the middle of five thousand man-hating women. I'd willingly walked into a man-hate festival. It was the longest hour and a half of my life, after church.

When the show let out we gave Angelica a ride back to her apartment. She lived in north Philadelphia.

"What did you think of the show?" Angelica asked me in the car.

"I was horrified by that karate routine," I confessed.

"I don't know," Angelica said. "I think it's high time women started fighting back. Men have always beaten women, haven't they?"

"Speak for your own friends. Don't you think that's fucked-up thinking? Some men are assholes so you blame the entire group. Isn't that what Hitler did?"

"I take it you didn't like the show, Tom?"

"That 'Fight Back' song really put me off. I don't believe in feeding into the cycle of violence."

Sterling said nothing. Angelica's apartment was in a quiet, shady neighborhood near one of the universities. Angelica had a small but comfortable efficiency on the second floor of an ivory-covered villa. It was really a very comfortable, cool apartment. She made tea. While we waited for tea Angelica went on about how women historically have been given the shaft.

"Do you know in the Jewish religion there's even a prayer men say thanking God they weren't born a woman?"

"Sure, in the Torah."

"Oh, then you're Jewish?" she asked me.

"No."

She seemed disappointed.

"But I grew up in a Jewish neighborhood," I threw in. "And of course I've been circumcised."

But close only counts with hand grenades and horseshoes. For a moment, when she thought I was a Jew, she'd seemed interested. Now she cooled off. She asked Sterling if she'd seen Hank lately.

"No," Sterling said. That was all.

I thought, Doesn't she realize Hank is history?

While she served tea Angelica showed us photographs of her father, a darling gray-haired old man who'd gone blind. There were pictures of Angelica leading the old guy around a summer beach house. Photographs of the old man walking by himself in the sand down by the surf. You could see how much she treasured him.

"You know," Angelica finally said to Sterling, "your little sister is nothing like you. She doesn't even look like you."

"Did everything go all right?" Sterling was guardedly aware of my presence. "I haven't had a chance to talk to Val."

"Yes everything went fine. But I just can't get over how much she's different from you."

"We travel in much different circles," Sterling said. "I can't stand her friends. You know, they'll sit around making jokes about 'queers and fags.'"

It was getting late. Angelica asked if we'd spend the night. Sterling shook her head no. We said friendly good-byes then hit the road. It was quiet for awhile but somewhere on the turnpike Sterling said I'd been right about the karate number. She didn't like violence either.

We started to fight about it. I don't know what got us started. I don't even know what we were arguing about. Maybe it was just because I hadn't had a very good evening. Quite suddenly though she turned to me and said softly, "I don't want to fight with you." She moved her jaw that way she had of doing.

I asked if she'd review the concert for the magazine. She shook her head no.

"It was a feminist event the men at the magazine wouldn't understand."

"What's there to understand?"

"I don't want to write something only to have some man who doesn't know what he's talking about change it all around."

"Don't worry," I told her. "I'm the damn editor. Hand in a review and no changes will be made."

All the next week she worked diligently, using my typewriter. We'd fixed up the middle room upstairs, covering the walls with posters from record albums, making it into an office. This by the way didn't sit well with Nicholson, whose house it was. He'd expected to come home from school on weekends and use the middle room to jump bimbos. But Sterling didn't want Nicholson around. She intimated that she might move out if Nicholson started showing up in the middle of the night with his menagerie of strange women. Faced with the choice of Sterling or Nicholson I sided with her. So one weekend when Nicholson showed up we told him we didn't want him around.

The three of us had a good row in his kitchen that night. Nicholson had been having a tough time attending school in Philadelphia. His first week in the city he'd witnessed a trolley disaster. A trolley had tipped over and crowds of people, hoping to collect insurance settlement money, came running to jump on the wreck. When the cops came an incredible mob — three or four hundred people — surrounded the trolley, trying to hold on, pretending they'd all been on the thing when it'd tipped over.

Nicholson felt alienated by the city. He'd gone so far as to seek counseling but, ever the tightwad, he'd sought a bargain rate. Some people, seeking a cheap haircut, will go to a barber school. Nicholson, lonely and dejected in the city, applied this discount idea to psychiatric care. He discovered he could get cheap counseling if he subjected himself to psychology students at the school of medicine. He went and cried his eyes out to some twenty-year-old kid. He poured his heart out, saying how lonely and lost he felt. The kid sat listening to him for the longest time. Then the student pulled out a medical text, paged through the thick book, finally hitting on what he thought was a pertinent passage.

"It says here you should learn to feed on your pain," he told Nicholson.

It was feeble advice but after all it'd only cost ten bucks. Making matters worse, he'd had his share of women problems. One day his ex-wife called him at his lonely room. She'd just come in from Ohio and could they get together at her hotel? He gladly complied. He went off rubbing his hands together, his hair neatly combed, wearing a fresh shirt, thinking she wanted to patch things up. Far from wanting to patch things up, she'd been seeing a shrink who'd recommended, as crucial to her therapy, that she look up Nicholson and unload on him all the things he'd done to torment her over the years. It might have been good therapy for her but it made a wreck of him.

We didn't help Nicholson's sense of alienation when we told him we didn't want him around. He got so mad he jacked up the rent fifty dollars.

Anyway, Sterling worked all week on her review in the room we'd appropriated from Nicholson. When she handed it in I was appalled to find she hadn't used any capital letters or punctuation marks. She'd spelled women with a y, "womyn," so there wouldn't be any "men" in it. She couldn't be reasoned with. I suggested slight changes, little things like capitalizing the sentences or sprinkling in a few periods or commas here or there. She'd have nothing to do with it. She said capital letters, commas, and periods were part of the tyranny men had brought into the world. She threatened to withdraw the review. She said this always happened whenever she worked with *men*. Finally I gave in. I said I wouldn't change a damn thing. I guess I wanted to prove to her that I wasn't like most men.

When the magazine came out everyone wanted to know what had happened to all the capital letters in Sterling's review. Things came to a head when Falstaff confronted me about it.

After I bought Falstaff's car he'd fallen into a drinking binge. He'd hole up all day in his house drinking. I thought I could get him out of his funk so I'd appointed him copy editor. There was an interesting complication to Falstaff's appointment. One day two complementary dinner passes came in the mail — a free dinner at a new greasy spoon opening outside town. "A totally new world of dining experience awaits you," the tickets read.

Falstaff, the old linebacker, got to the mail first, intercepting the tickets. Nancy Downs, the priest killer and editor seductress, found out about it and called Falstaff, inviting herself along. Falstaff's new position must have appealed to her. Nicholson, since we'd kicked him out of his own house, meanwhile had taken a weekend room with Falstaff. The evening of Falstaff's big date with Nancy Downs I was in the office working late. Through the thin wall I could hear Falstaff and Nicholson talking. Falstaff, in preparation for his totally new world of dining experience with Nancy Downs, wore a suit and tie and plenty of cologne. Nicholson, finding this hilarious, rode him.

"You want to fuck Nancy Downs. Admit it," I heard Nicholson yell. The wall was very thin and I could hear every word.

"I have no such idea in mind." Falstaff really tried to sound indignant.

"Then what's with the suit and the cologne?"

"I thought I'd look nice for the totally new world of dining experience."

"Bullshit. I know you Falstaff. And I certainly know Nancy Downs."

Nicholson had once been an editor of the magazine. During his tenure as editor he had a fling with Nancy Downs. The thought of Falstaff and Nancy Downs was too much for his imagination. He laughed and laughed and laughed. They certainly deserve each other, I thought. I tried to put it out of my mind. I have no idea what happened on their date, and whether it truly was a totally new world of dining experience.

Anyway, Falstaff returned the favor of my naming him copy editor by trying to take my job away from me. He resented my being named editor ahead of him. He seized on Sterling's review as a means of getting my job. The day the magazine came back from the printer he buttonholed me in the layout room.

"Why wasn't this copy edited, Tom?" He waved Sterling's review in my face.

"That's the way Sterling wanted it."

"I got your number, Tom."

"What do you mean?"

"You've been pussywhipped!"

"What?"

"You were pussywhipped by that woman. Admit it. You live with her. Everyone knows what's been going on."

"What's been going on?"

"Oh I've got your number, Parker!" He got up from the

table. "I wonder what the editorial board will say about this. I've got your number, all right. You've gone too far this time. You've made your last mistake. You've allowed yourself to be pussywhipped by a woman who subverted the established editorial practices of this magazine. You're going to lose your job over this." He stormed from the room.

So now I was feuding with Falstaff. True to his word, he brought up the matter at the next editorial board meeting. He said they should dismiss me as editor and that he should have the job. It was a pretty spirited meeting. In the end Nancy Downs and the others on the board who were always against me voted against me. The people on the board who were always for me voted for me. Luckily I held the majority on the board. Democracy had vindicated me. Falstaff had overplayed his hand.

I was still editor. My first act was to fire Falstaff. Rather, he became an editor-without-portfolio. He sulked back to his house to deal with his bottle, while I sulked back to my house to deal with Sterling.

14.

Early in January Sterling drove to Washington to spend a weekend at a friend's apartment. Her friend was going out of town and had asked Sterling to house-sit. So she went down to DC to take in the museums. She took along Goldeneye, her Irish setter, leaving me with Godwit, the German shepherd.

That Saturday morning about nine o'clock I got a phone call from her.

"Why don't you come down here?" she asked. "There's a coffee pot. And a place for us to stay."

I didn't know what to say.

"Should I?"

"Well why don't you think about it. I'll call back in a little while. Okay?"

But she never called back. The moment I hung up I knew I'd made a mistake. I hung around the house all day waiting for the call that never came.

That weekend with the German shepherd passed slowly. We sat around the lonely place listening to every creak the house made. Whenever a siren went by he'd lift back his head and let off the most lonesome howl. At nights he'd become afraid.

He'd cry and scratch at my door and I'd have to let him in. He'd lie across the foot of my bed, at my feet.

Sunday night, when Sterling came home, the big German shepherd went crazy for the Irish setter. But the setter fought him off. "That's my girl," Sterling told Goldeneye. "Tell him to leave you alone." Godwit always went crazy if he was separated from Goldeneye for any length of time, Sterling said. He'd pine for the setter, climbing all over her when she returned. His advances fought off, Godwit lay down in a corner and sighed. I felt bad for him.

Later, Godwit got up, and Goldeneye came over. The bitch climbed on his back. As if in mockery of his desire she pretended to hump him.

15.

We typeset the magazine at a farm run by hippies in the country. The farm had been bought by an heiress whose family owned a Chicago newspaper. The heiress had come East with her husband during the back-to-nature days at the end of the Vietnam War. She was a rich Catholic hippie girl who came East to be a hanger-on when the group of radical priests went on trial, the priests supposedly plotting to kidnap Henry Kissinger. During the trial the heiress housed other, less fortunate hippie hangers-on at her farm. There was a big, beautiful stone farmhouse, several nice outbuildings, and about fifty acres of woods. The radical priests would come to the farm and hold secret masses out in the woods for the heiress and the other hangers-on. I'd heard wild stories of police in helicopters all the time spying on the farm, of hippies running naked through fields while radical priests celebrated mass in the woods.

At any given time there might be twenty hangers-on living at the farm and abusing the heiress' hospitalities. A lot of the hippies on the farm were running from something — probably the law. Most had spurious hippie names, like Desertflower

Jack, Sunshine Mary and Happy Humanist. Happy Humanist was a soft-spoken, shaggy man. Once I asked him why he called himself Happy Humanist. He said it was because his real name was Richard.

"What does that have to do with it?"

"I don't like the phallic implications of being called Dick."

Another of the hangers-on was a big, middle-aged man who called himself Isiah. Isiah's round face was ground zero for a great explosion of hair and beard. Later I found out Isiah was actually a former insurance executive whose real name was Bernard Kauffman or something similarly middle class, and who apparently was on the lam from the law in New England. I'd been typesetting one day when I got bored and started asking Isiah about his background. When he got to the part where he'd been forced to leave his insurance business he clammed up.

"There was nothing to it, nothing to it at all," he said, upset, desiring to change the subject.

Before long Isiah and the heiress began to have an affair. They weren't too private about it. Finally the heiress' husband moved out from the big farmhouse into a little outbuilding, where he pursued his job and hobby of making guns. As soon as the husband was out of the way Isiah convinced the heiress she should give up ownership of the farm and sign it over to humanity in the form of a land trust. The heiress finally relented, but not before her husband divorced her. Saying he wasn't about to sign *his* half of the farm over to humanity, he broke up the farm and kept the half with his gun shop. The heiress' former husband continued to live on the premises.

The trouble with the land trust turned out to be that humanity was a negligent caretaker. Humanity never paid any bills. The heiress still had to underwrite the farm. The hippies tried all kinds of wacky schemes to raise money independent of the heiress. A free school. Seminars in new-age topics. Even a magazine on land trusts. Isiah bought expensive typesetting equipment and set up a type shop in one of the outbuildings. He'd rent time to outsiders for extremely reasonable rates — that's why we came to the farm. At the time the magazine was too poor to afford its own typesetting equipment. We used to have IBM equipment but we couldn't afford the payments and had to let it go.

"Such a little company at the mercy of such a big company," Jenkins, my reporter friend at the capitol newsroom, used to moan.

It was almost a half-hour drive to the farm but Isiah's typesetting rates were so low it made it worthwhile. Often Nate Freeman and I would go together. We'd make a nice day of it in the country, taking turns setting type and walking through the lush green farm. Freeman was a great typist and typesetter. He'd fly along at eighty-five words a minute, editing sloppy copy as he went. He seldom made a typo but when he did he'd momentarily stop and say "Screw."

One day, before he went to Philadelphia on his GI Bill, Nicholson drove down to the farm with Freeman and me. Nicholson didn't come along to help typeset. He was notoriously late handing in his copy. He'd wait till the last possible minute then drive along with us so he could finish his article even while we set the rest of the magazine. Nicholson brought along a heavy old Remington typewriter, one of those old-fashioned jobs that weigh a ton and you can look in and see all the rods, levers and moving parts. Freeman's car was pretty full, so Nicholson had to sit in the front seat with the bulky old typewriter on his lap.

Halfway to the farm Freeman was pulled over by a cop in a routine check. Nicholson was annoyed by the delay. Rolling a sheet of paper into the typewriter he asked the cop for his name and badge number. The cop looked into the car and saw Nicholson in the front passenger's seat typing away on his big old Remington. Nicholson snarled we were investigative reporters doing a story on traffic cops. The cop's eyes bugged out. He let us go. Before we got to the farm we stopped at a restaurant for coffee. Nicholson, seeing a row of motorcycles parked out front, made it a point to hide the typewriter, saying he didn't want to be pegged as a literati by the bikers, as he might get beat up.

Late one night I went typesetting with Jack Falstaff. We drove down in the middle of the night, taking Falstaff's car, the one he'd eventually sell to me. Due at the printer by noon, we furiously set type until five in the morning. It was a very cold, dark night, and as we pulled out of the farm's gravel driveway we got a flat. We couldn't loosen the bolts on the tire. Falstaff only had one of those crummy Volkswagen tube wrenches. We knew it'd be hopeless to go back to the farm because all the hippies were asleep. Besides, Falstaff's Audi used metric tools and there was nothing on the farm but old American clunkers. It was about five miles over dark windy roads to the nearest gas station.

"Do you think we should try driving on the flat?" Falstaff asked.

"It's your car," I told him.

The dark dead of cold winter night. Falstaff started out for the gas station on the flat tire. He drove the car slowly, his great bulk squeezed behind the steering wheel. We got amazingly far on the flat, up over the hills, winding along the dark landscape at fifteen miles an hour. At last we reached the ramp to the expressway. I was worried that the flat tire might overheat. As we came to the expressway ramp I saw a little patch of snow, and suggested to Falstaff that a drive through the snow might cool the tire. He complied. A great cloud of steam billowed from the wheel. The sudden cooling caused the tire to smoke.

Falstaff got mad. He tried to blame the whole thing on me.

"Sure," I said to him, "I held a gun to your head and made

you drive five miles on a flat tire."

We wound slowly up the highway ramp, a great smelly cloud pouring from the wheel. The car bounced all around. Falstaff, his anger growing, followed the shoulder up a hill. Suddenly he stopped the car. He sat trembling behind the wheel. I was afraid to say anything. I really thought he might belt me.

I got out of the car and walked over the crest of the hill. A service station, and an all-night store sat just on the other side. I trudged back to Falstaff. He'd cooled off some. We drove the car over the hill, parking in front of the gas station's bay doors. The instant we pulled in the flat tire self-destructed. The rubber became undone and rolled off the metal hub. The tread lay bare on the asphalt.

The gas station turned out to be closed till seven. It was now a little before six. We walked over to the all-night store. The attendant, I swear to God, was a pinhead. He was as big and stupid as Zippy. We asked him if he had a metric tire iron in his car.

"Yes," he replied. "In my trunk."

There was a pregnant silence.

"Well, do you think we can borrow it?"

"No. I never loan out tools."

Falstaff and I resigned ourselves. What could we do? We bought coffee and Tastykakes and stood around the empty store watching the pinhead and joking about the crap the store was selling. We could hear the birds of morning starting to sing. The sun was coming up. Falstaff was no longer mad. He got philosophical, saying there was nothing to do until the gas station opened at seven. The pinhead did nothing the whole time but wipe the counter. We killed time reading the headlines on the scandal sheets.

"'Illinois man commits unspeakable offense,'" I read to Falstaff.

"What did he do?"
"I don't know. It was unspeakable."
"That's right. It's an unspeakable offense."
"You can't speak about an unspeakable offense."
"That's right. It's unspeakable."
"We shouldn't even be speaking about it now."
"Certainly you're right. That's why it's unspeakable."

The pinhead looked up from wiping the counter.

"You two look like you don't have a care in the world," he said.

What could we say? Next the pinhead announced he had to go out and read the meters on his gas pumps. He didn't want to leave the two of us alone in the store. We might steal all the Twinkies. He made us go out with him and stand by the gas pumps while he read the meters.

Finally seven o'clock rolled around. A mechanic in a pickup bounced into the gas station across the street. We said goodbye to the pinhead, walked back to the car.

The mechanic wasn't happy. He asked if that was our car parked in front of his service bay. We said it was. He snarled that his insurance didn't allow broken-down cars to be left on his property.

"Excuse our ignorance," Falstaff told him. "We should have known better than to leave a broken car at a service station."

Falstaff decided he'd play a joke on the mechanic. He'd found one of those little plastic screw-on caps that goes over the tire's air valve. He bounced after the mechanic into the garage. With a straight face he showed the mechanic the little cap off the tire valve.

"This came off," he told the mechanic. He handed over the little black cap. "Do you think this has anything to do with the problem?"

The mechanic took in the valve cap, then the decimated tire, the rubber curled beside it on the pavement.

"No, that don't got nothing to do with it."

He didn't know what to make of Falstaff and me. He quickly got out his power wrench, changed the tire and we were on our way. We weren't even late for the printer.

All this happened in the days when the heiress still lived on the farm where we would go to typeset. After awhile the heiress took Isiah on a trip to Europe. Shortly thereafter she ditched him for another man in Calcutta. After she ditched Isiah the heiress never returned to the farm. Humanity truly was left to look after the farm then and some truly strange characters moved in, including boat people of all nationalities and a tribe of fake Indians — white men — who'd departed an Indian reservation in a hurry and had to beat it to the farm to hide out.

A few weeks after I was named editor I got a mysterious phone call from Nancy Downs, my nemesis on the editorial board. It was a Saturday afternoon.

"I don't have anything to do today," she said. "I thought maybe I'd go typesetting with you at the farm."

"Typesetting? With me?"

"You are going typesetting today, aren't you?"

"Yes."

"I'd like to come with you. Unless you have some objection. I thought maybe you could use some help."

"Sure. Why not."

She picked me up at the office. We drove down to the farm together, talking small talk. It was a nice fall day in the country. The last of the butterflies and grasshoppers were cavorting in the tall brown grass. We spent most of the afternoon typesetting in the little outbuilding. We got a lot done. I'd set an article then take a break, go outside and sit in the sun while Nancy Downs took over.

Toward the end of the afternoon she came out and sat in the sun with me. She'd brought along one of those carryall bags you get from giving money to public TV. Opening the bag, she took out two apples, a small wheel of cheese and a knife. She cut off pieces of apple and cheese and gave them to me. I don't think I've described her at all. She had short black hair, the bangs cut squarely at the eyebrows. She wasn't what you'd call beautiful but she had a handsome, almost impish face and a well-formed body. Everything she did told you she was sure of herself.

Suddenly, sitting in the grass, she leaned back and said, "It's so hard sometimes to be a woman."

I said nothing.

She sat up.

"Over there, in the woods," she said, pointing with the knife, "that's where I first made love with my former husband."

"The priest?"

"Yes, the former priest."

"Too bad about what happened to him."

"Yes. It was too bad."

"Too bad about John Baines."

"Yes it was too bad about him too."

"He must have been delicate."

"Yes Baines was very delicate."

"But not as delicate as the priest, I suppose."

"No. The priest was very delicate. He was the one who insisted on marrying, you know. I could have had it either way. He and the other priests, when they were on trial, used to come out here and say mass in the woods, you know. There's a boulder they used as an altar. That's where the priest and I first made love. Should I show it to you?"

I looked at my watch.

"I don't know, Nancy. I don't have much time."

"Maybe some other time."

"Yes. Some other time."

Again she leaned back and said it was difficult to be a woman.

"You'll never know," she said.
"Sometimes it's tough to be a man too."
She said nothing.
I went back in and finished typesetting. On the ride back to town we had a pleasant conversation. Before she let me out she asked if I cared to have dinner. I was busy, I reminded her.
"Can I give you a ride home?"
"No. But thanks anyway."

Winter dragged on. One evening I had to set type with the magazine's art director and I talked Sterling into coming along. I told Sterling she'd enjoy meeting the art director. He was a serious artist whose name was Roger Henley. He'd spent a good number of years trying to make it as an artist in New York City. But finally the lack of recognition and the lack of money had led him to the brink of suicide.

One lonely night in Manhattan he'd finally decided to kill himself. He'd strung the phone cord over a rafter and had his neck in the makeshift noose when two persistent Seventh Day Adventists came pounding on his door. They saved his life. They hadn't converted him or anything like that. It had taken all the gumption he could muster to put his head through the noose and when they'd disturbed him he had to get down off the chair, answer the door and scream at them to get lost. Couldn't they see he was trying to kill himself? The two Seventh Day Adventists saw the chair under the swinging noose. They ran off in terror. It was so funny Henley began to laugh and after that he didn't want to kill himself anymore.

Anyway, Sterling at first said she didn't want to go typesetting with us. Henley and I were about ready to leave the office for the farm when Sterling came walking though the darkness. She'd changed her mind. The three of us rode out into the country in Henley's car. The whole way Sterling and Henley talked. We parked and silently walked down through the snowy trees to the darkened print shop. It was the dead of winter, a frigid night, but there was a big moon lighting everything up in that way moonlight has on snow. It was so cold that the snow was as hard and crunchy as styrofoam, with slippery spots of ice here and there, so that you had to walk carefully. Sterling moved silently between us, her hands buried deep in her parka pockets. We spent several hours setting type. It was an enjoyable evening.

The next night, while I was working in the layout room, I talked with Henley about women. He was a great one to talk with about women. Women always hung around his art studio, throwing themselves at him, wanting to pose for him. Once Henley told me I should, before I died, make love to a woman much taller than I.

"Why?"

"You've never done it until you've done it with a woman who's bigger than you."

Now Henley got me talking about Sterling.

"She's driving me crazy," I confessed. "And I don't have anyone to talk to about it. All my close friends are away at school."

"Well what's bugging you Tom?"

"I don't know if she wants me or not."

"It sounds like you're in love with her."

"I don't know."

"Have you slept with her yet?"

"No. It's a tricky affair. The other day she called me from DC. I thought she wanted me to come down and spend the weekend but then she backed off. I think it's maybe because I'm her roommate. She doesn't want to complicate things with me."

"Sounds like you're getting a lot of mixed signals."

Just then Sterling came in and we had to break off the conversation. She stayed well into the night, helping us lay out pages.

The next morning, back at the house, I told her about my conversation with Henley.

"What? You mean you were *talking* about our relationship with someone else?"

"Is that what this is? He simply asked me if I ever slept with you."

"What? I can't believe people go around asking you things like that, Tom. You're the only one in the world who people ask these things. Nobody ever asks me if I've slept with so and so."

"Why not?"

"Because it's nobody else's damn business, that's why."

She was standing in the kitchen doorway with her hand on her hip. She kept moving her jaw in that funny way she had. "Henley has all the nerve. I have a good mind not to go over to his house tonight."

"What?"

"The other night, when we were out typesetting, he asked me over to his apartment to watch Shakespeare on television. Now I don't know if I'll go."

"When did he ask you this?"

"I don't know. When you were in the bathroom or something."

"Well how do you like that! You're not going, are you?"

"I don't know. I haven't made up my mind."

That night when I came home Sterling wasn't there. I went out walking. I walked for the longest time through the snow. When I got back Sterling still wasn't home. I closed the door to my room and slept.

The next morning when I got up Sterling sat in the kitchen drinking coffee and eating homemade yogurt. She said she wanted to go skiing before all the snow melted.

"Really?" I said. "Can I come with?"

"I don't know, Tom. You said you don't know how to ski.

You won't be able to keep up with me."

"Why don't we go snow camping? You brought your tent but we still haven't gone."

She said nothing. For going on a month her two-man tent had been sitting by the front door. I'd see it every time I'd go out. I let the conversation drop.

Later that day when I was at the office I happened to look out the window and saw Sterling's truck pull up on Third Street. Two sets of skis were tied to her truck cap. Our intern Pete got out of the truck, waved, then trudged through the snow to the office. He came in, announced he'd just been skiing. Seeing me, he fell quiet. He proceeded to walk around the office like a bantam rooster, his shoulders stiff and arrogant.

"Why don't you get to work on your article," I told him. "Deadline's tomorrow at five."

16.

A few days later Sterling's friend Angelica came for a visit. I drove them out into the country in my car. I drove fast, without saying much, watching Angelica's long thick hair lift in the wind as we blew down the road. We spent the evening playing Scrabble at a friend's house. Afterwards we drove home and sat together talking at the kitchen table. Before long Sterling and Angelica excused themselves. They went up to Sterling's room, closed the door. It was the quiet still of night. I restlessly walked over to the office and worked all night.

I didn't get back to the house until the next afternoon. Sterling wasn't home. I put on a record. I sat down at the kitchen table. I poured myself a glass of wine. After awhile I heard the front door rattle. Sterling came in with her dogs.

"Where were you, Tom?"

"I spent the night working at the office. Where's Angelica?"

"She went home."

Sterling sat down at the kitchen table.

"Wine?"

"Thanks."

She made that funny motion with her jaw.

"Angelica was afraid you were angry with her and that's why you left."

"Angry? Why should I be angry with Angelica?"

"She thought you may have minded us sleeping together." I drank some wine.

"I really don't care who you sleep with," I said. "I'll win you in the end. I'm the only one who understands you."

Sterling stood, threw her scarf to the table.

"You're so damn confident of yourself. What gives you the right?"

17.

The snows that winter were the deepest they'd been in years. In early February it snowed heavily three times in one week. The plows had trouble making headway. Things got worse when the over-worked, under-maintained snow plows started breaking down. After a week the snow really started piling up. The mayor, slightly drunk, called together department heads for a late-night meeting. Hizzoner handed out shovels, suggesting the department heads go out and heave to it.
  In early February it got so bad cars were abandoned altogether. The blizzard got so wild and white even the buses quit running. I was downtown, in my heavy parka and good mountaineering boots, and had to huff it all the way up Second Street, stopping every few feet to help push cars from snow banks. When I got home Sterling sat wistfully on the kitchen table, her legs crossed.
  "I can't wait for summer," she said, bouncing her crossed leg, her hands propping her up behind her. "You know what I really like? Hot hair." She laughed, running her hands now through her hair. She said to her setter, "Maybe we should set the living room on fire, Goldeneye, so I can have hot hair."

About this time Sterling seemed to have a fierce yearning for an earlier, simpler time in her life. She began calling friends from years in the past, back before she'd known the feminists and the lesbians, the radicals and the artists at the magazine. One day she called a fellow she'd worked with at the army depot. He came dressed for a date. He was surprised to find me in the kitchen.

"This is my housemate," Sterling told him. We shook hands. He was a husky fellow, with a thick face. And a beard. He seemed nice enough.

They went out drinking. Hours later Sterling came home alone. It was after midnight when she came in. I was up in the middle room typing. She came up and sat beside me on the desk.

"What do you say?"

"I say, I wish my hair was hot," she said. She ruffled her hair with her hands. She laughed.

"I believe you're drunk."

"Uh-huh."

"Well did you have a nice time?"

"Yes. But Rod's such a bore."

"He seemed all right to me."

"I don't know why I called him. I guess it was because of all the fun we used to have back at the depot. We all ran around in a crowd. I guess Rod reminds me of that."

The next weekend another of Sterling's old chums came to visit. This time it was a woman named Violet. Like Rod, Violet had also worked with Sterling at the army depot, ordering parts for weapons. She was a tall woman with a ready, loud laugh. Violet had just been to Seattle. She talked of rebuffing married men in the bars of the hotels where she stayed. While she was out there she'd hooked up with Nate Freeman, at Sterling's suggestion. She told us how he was. Violet really didn't know what to make of Freeman. She worked for some government agency in DC and all her men were responsible office types, which Freeman certainly was not.

By listening to Violet's conversation I inadvertently learned it was her apartment Sterling had house-sat in DC.

"Were you alone the whole weekend?" Violet asked.

"No. Hank came down." That was all she said. She seemed guarded. The subject was changed.

We made dinner for Violet. Our guest was impressed by my prowess in the kitchen. While we ate I played Bob Dylan's Blonde on Blonde album. When it got to Just Like a Woman Sterling looked up from her plate.

"This is a dumb song."

"Oh I don't know," I said. "I like it."

"I hate the line about breaking just like a little girl. He wrote so many good songs but that's detestable."

Sterling let it drop. I got this feeling there were aspects of her life she didn't want her old working buddy to know about. After dinner I put on the television. There was a movie on public TV about a woman in the old West who'd run away from her husband. She'd moved in with another woman and the two evidently had become lovers, or as close to lovers as two women can get on public TV. In the end the husband showed up and took his wife away. Men always ruin things, one of the women said to the other. I was just getting interested when Sterling uncomfortably switched off the television.

Later that week Sterling, out for a walk, was bitten by a dog. It wasn't a bad bite. Just a little flesh wound around her ankle. A little shook up, she called me at the office and told me about it. "I feel so stupid. I've been bit by a dog." I went to meet her at the hospital. When she came from the examining room her shirt was unbuttoned and you could partially see her breast. I moved my hand to her button. Pulling away, she went back into the examining room to button her own shirt.

Not long after that it was my birthday. Sterling had gone to see her folks for the weekend. So there I was alone on my birthday. It got to be pretty late, ten or eleven o'clock at night. I sat drinking. I heard a key slide into the lock. The door opened. The dogs bounced in, followed by Sterling. I was sitting at the kitchen table.

She came in with a homemade cake. Peanut butter icing. She set it on the table.

"Well, Sterling, what do you say?"

Bending in front of me she kissed me on the lips.

"I say, Happy birthday."

18.

My life was starting to feel shaky, like a wobbly table that wild forces presently might overthrow. Whether Sterling was a force of stability or instability I couldn't say, though she seemed to me as predictable as a cyclone.

As winter wore on strange things began to happen around town. One day at the airport a man announced he'd fly a balloon across the ocean to Europe. With much fanfare he waved to the cameras, kissed his wife good-bye, climbed into his gondola, and sailed away into the gray clouds, never to be seen or heard from again. Everyone suspected he'd gone down in the ocean.

And of course we were all shocked when we lost half our fire department in the truly bizarre hole incident. A couple of boys had been messing around a deep sinkhole at the edge of the mountains. Over the years the neighbors had taken to dumping leaves into the hole. Quite a pile of leaves had accumulated. One of the boys decided to jump in, believing the leaves would break his fall. How could he have known the decaying leaves had filled the hole with methane gas? He quickly passed out. His friend ran for help.

Someone called the rescue ambulance. The ambulance was

manned by three brothers who were well liked around town. One brother jumped into the hole, whereupon, in the soft leaves, he wobbled and keeled over. Seeing this, one of his brothers jumped in, but he too keeled over. So naturally the third brother jumped in.

Soon two or three police cars, another rescue ambulance, a fire truck and a mobile TV unit were on the scene.

"The Landry brothers have gone down in the hole!" one of the firemen yelled. He quick grabbed his hat, jumped in, followed by all of Fire Company 54, four policeman, a school crossing guard and the second rescue unit.

A madness had come over our firemen. Without stopping to think grown men came running and flung themselves into the hole, piling up on each other. Scarcely had one conked out before another jumped in. The hole quickly filled. If the hole had been big enough the whole state might have jumped in.

This came to be known as the Great Sinkhole Catastrophe. We lost many fine firemen that terrible day, though most curiously the boy who started it all survived. He'd evidently passed out in an air pocket and was able to breathe. After the firemen were cleared off he was lifted to freedom.

Not long after that some elementary school kids had their fingers ripped off in an equally bizarre incident. A gigantic tug-of-war, involving twelve hundred kids, had been organized at the city junior high. The telephone company donated a thick steel cable.

The children lined up in the school field, each taking hold of the cable. When a whistle blew they groaned and strained, pulling each other back and forth. Tremendous tension built up in the cable. Suddenly it gave way, the pent-up energy driving the cable like a wild snapping whip, almost as if it had come alive. It lashed off the fingers of a dozen or so kids. Children ran screaming as the mad cable snaked around the field with an unearthly whooshing sound.

One evening late in March my friends Tony and Beth stopped by. They were on their way home from the movies. They'd just seen a movie about an errant atomic power plant. Tony said the movie reminded him of his stint in the navy. He'd been a navy photographer during the Cuban Missile Crisis. At the height of the crisis he'd been ordered to photograph the buildings in Washington. Someone in power thought the monuments might soon be gone.

"I just got the same sort of creepy feeling at the movies," he said.

He stood there in his ratty old gray Goodwill overcoat, clutching his ratty Goodwill hat between his hands in front of him, his ratty beard trembling. "Tom. I'm telling you. I was *scared.*" At the time I didn't think much of it. Now when I look back I see his nervous visit as a foreshadowing of things to come.

19.

The next morning I went early to the office. The magazine had just come back from the printer and the issue had to be mailed out. I'd given the job to Pete, the intern. He was supposed to have met me there, but he was a no show. I was sorting through the bundles when I got a call from Jenkins at the capitol newsroom.

"There's been a leak of some kind down at the nuclear reactor. I thought you'd like to know. You've been following it and all."

"What kind of leak?"

"I don't know. It just came over the wire. I just thought you'd like to know."

"Thanks, Jenks."

He hung up.

Pete, the intern, came in, apologizing for his lateness. On the way to work he'd dallied at a street festival. Rushing around looking for my notepad, I told him there'd been some kind of leak at the reactor.

"Mind if I go back to the street festival?" he said. "I think it'd make a nice story."

"Fuck the street festival. I said there's been a leak at the reactor."

Pete hmmed and hahhed. He really wanted to go to the street festival. I didn't argue. This was the guy who couldn't see anything wrong with locking up fire extinguishers.

I drove through thick early morning traffic down river to the gate of the reactor. Already a wire photographer was on hand, standing in front of the guard box, casually snapping pictures.

"What's going on?" I asked.

"Search me. They just sent me out."

The plant's four cooling towers dominated the background. The reactors occupied an island in a pretty bend in the river. We used to have to pass the nuclear plant when we took the magazine to the printer, just down the river. The colossal size of the two reactors always took you by surprise.

I went up to the guard box. The guard inside seemed cagey.

"What's going on?"

"I don't know."

A dosimeter hung on his lapel.

"What's that thing say?"

He looked down brusquely.

"It's not important now."

Cars began streaming from the plant. A long line of cars came snaking off the island. They stopped at the main gate by the guardhouse. Two technicians hurried out, sweeping Geiger counters over each car.

It made you think this wasn't such a good place to hang out. The main gate opened, the cars streamed out. They came one after another to the highway and turned right, wasting no time, tires spinning in the gravel. I heard one of the drivers say to another, "We're all supposed to go to the substation down the road to be tested for contamination."

One of the cars stopped at the road. I yelled over, asking if this was a drill.

"No. This ain't no drill."
"Then it's a shift change?"
"No. Now excuse me bud."

He rolled up his window, took off after the others. Forty or fifty cars streamed from the plant, stopped momentarily to be swept by Geiger counters at the gate, then barreled up the road out of sight. All the while the cooling towers hung in the background.

Some sort of wild frightening premonition swept over me. The idea came to me to put five hundred miles between me and this place. I turned and started back to my car. I only took two or three steps, then I stopped. Maybe I should call some friends, I thought. Let them know the reactor's about to melt. It would be a kind, a thoughtful thing to do, a kindness I'd appreciate from a friend. But I wouldn't be able to reach most of the people I knew.

For a minute I stood watching the chaos. More reporters started showing up. I remembered reading that Mencken had cut his teeth on the great Baltimore fire. Gathering myself, I suggested to a few of the reporters that we split up, interview the neighbors living around the plant, then report back in fifteen minutes. We all went different ways. I interviewed an old couple working in their yard. I came up their lawn and asked if they knew what was going on. Both shook their heads, said they had no idea anything was wrong. In front of their home cars streamed bumper to bumper from the plant.

"Isn't it a drill?" the old man said. He was standing there with a rake. The old woman asked me if I cared for some tea.

I met the other reporters back at the gate.

"These people don't know anything about what's going on."
"None of these people have been told anything."

A reporter from the local daily paper showed up. He got out of his car in his tweed jacket, taking in the procession of cars leaving the plant.

"What's going on here?" he yelled over.

"It doesn't take a rocket scientist to see there's something wrong with this picture."

I jumped in my car and joined the procession up the road.

20.

I drove like a shot up to a little A-frame that had been built across the river from the reactor. The A-frame served as a tourist observation center. In quieter times people could come and look at posters and displays of Our Friend the Atom. Now helicopters carrying utility executives and network TV reporters spun down on the back lawn. I parked my car by the side of the road and hurried across the lawn. At the house next door little children played on a swing while, on the lawn at the front of the observation center, a team of dour radiation specialists came urgently by, sweeping the air and grass with Geiger counters.

"Team alpha to team beta," one of their walkie-talkies kept squawking. "Now sweeping the southeast quadrant of the island."

Six or seven sullen plant workers sat at picnic tables calmly eating lunch. They watched smoke billow from a small stack near the reactor.

I went up to the table.

"What's going on? Is something wrong?"

"Even if there was what makes you think you could understand it?" one of them barked back.

They were eyeing my camera and tape recorder. No use making people freeze up. I ran back to the car and threw my reporter's gear in the trunk. I returned to the observation center and went inside. Plant workers huddled in small knots, nervously talking to each other in excited whispers. Two men sat whispering under a poster of Reddy Kilowatt. The one man's hands shook so badly I had to wonder if I'd made the right decision to stay. I wandered up to the second level. A wild-faced foreman burst out of a side room waving a clipboard, looking worried, not even trying to maintain composure.

"There's been a mix up somewhere here!" he yelled.

There was too much confusion for anyone to notice me. I went into a side room hoping to overhear something. Excited workers blabbed gibberish to each other. No one was listening. They were just the backward characters of my hometown, now with an atomic age problem dropped in laps better meant for bass fishing. I heard somebody say a company vice president had just touched down in a helicopter out back.

I went out for a look, sliding downstairs and out the back door. A man in a blue three-piece suit had just convened a press conference on the back lawn. Helicopter rotor blades spun behind him while radiation teams swept the grass.

"Team alpha to team beta! Now sweeping the southwest quadrant of the island!"

"This was just a small mishap," the utility executive told a circle of reporters. He was almost drowned out by the radiation teams sweeping the grass around him. "Everything's under control. It was a normal anomaly. Just a little water spilt on the floor, that's all. The reactor will be shut down for a few weeks, I'd imagine." He made it sound like they were in there mopping things up now.

While he spoke the radiation teams fanned out, sweeping all around us, the grass, the trees, the buildings. Several reporters, not knowing much about radiation, asked the executive to compare the amount of radioactive water that had been spilled on the floor to a dental x-ray.

"Is this a meltdown?" I broke in.

The executive froze. Saying nothing, he hurried away inside the A-frame.

I went around to the front of the observation center. State policemen stationed out front had just been issued dosimeters. A cardboard box full of the tube-like radiation measuring devices had been dropped on the side of the road. The cops were distributing them among themselves. They had no idea how to use them. One trooper pointed his dosimeter at the ground, twisting it like it was a kaleidoscope. Out front a line of reporters had already gathered at a pay phone to call in stories. I had to stand in line nearly twenty minutes. When it was my turn I called the office and asked Sam, our community reporter, to hurry over with a couple stacks of the magazine in which the spontaneous human combustion expert had predicted a meltdown. Twenty minutes didn't go by when here came Sam and his buddy Max, dressed in his customary Hawaiian shirt, hauling a trunkload of the meltdown issue, which we wasted no time passing out to surprised reporters.

21.

I drove home later that afternoon feeling satisfied about things. It had been an interesting way to spend an afternoon. On the way home I passed four or five anti-nuclear demonstrators protesting in front of the governor's mansion. They urgently held signs up to the rush-hour traffic. "Do you know there was a major accident today at the nuclear reactor?" the signs read in hurried scrawl. Nervous cranks. When I got to the house Sterling huddled over the radio in the kitchen.
"Something happened today at the reactor," she said.
"Yeah, I know. I just came from there. Some sort of leak. They say they've got it under control."
"It may be worse than they're letting on. I've been listening to a news conference down at the capitol. It's still leaking radiation. Nobody seems to know if the leaks are accidental or intentional."
"I'm sure they have things under control."
I caught a quick bite then walked to the office to work on the mailing. I was just finishing up when I got a phone call from a frantic out-of-town anti-nuclear activist. The accident was much worse than the utility executives were letting on, she

insisted. She begged me to get out of town, pleaded with me to come stay at her house, a hundred miles away. "Bring as many people as you can!" I'd never met this woman yet she was offering me a place to stay.

The call left me a little spooked. I was alone at the office. It was about nine at night. I called Jenkins down at the capitol newsroom.

"Listen, Parker, there's nothing to worry about. The accident's over. That's what everybody in a position of responsibility is saying. That woman's been calling everyone in the newsroom all night, talking to anyone who'll listen. We've been ignoring her. So should you."

Lucky for me the local anti-nukes had their small office in the same building as the magazine. I went downstairs. The anti-nukes were busy. Before the accident they'd had a dozen members. Now volunteers drifted in off the street. Reporters filtered in and out. One of the anti-nukes wanted a ride to their meetinghall, where they were drafting a letter to the governor. I had nothing better to do so I gave him a lift.

The meetinghall was jumping. People painted posters in one room while in another they worked on their letter to the governor. They wanted to say that the situation was worse than the utility was letting on, but they couldn't find the language. Another reporter and I sat for a half an hour listening to an old man rewrite the first line innumerable times. Impatient, the other reporter finally grabbed the typewriter and finished the letter. Then four or five of us took off in my car looking for a Xerox machine. By the time we got to the governor's mansion a sizable group of protesters had gathered. Inside the mansion gates offical cars jammed the parking lot.

A man who was missing several front teeth flitted here and there through the crowd whispering, "The governor's meeting with the feds. Expect a cover-up."

I spotted the president of the local anti-nuclear group. A

very prim and proper little white-haired man, brimming with rectitude, he worked the crowd asking for a ride downtown, to the emergency preparedness office. He was about sixty years old, wearing a suit and tie, a former school teacher.

"Ask him," someone pointed at me. "He's got a car."

The old man came up.

"How about it? Can you give me a ride?"

"Well I just got here myself."

"Please. It's important."

I gave in. We got into the car and drove down the quiet riverfront. The sky was turning red. At the courthouse I parked, followed him in.

The civil defense office was bedlam. People rushed everywhere. The civil defense director swam in paper and plans. He was a young man with thick blond hair and a harried, nervous demeanor. This job wasn't much good for his health. He stood wearily at the counter, yelling over two telephones. Finally he shouldered the phones.

"Where are your evacuation plans?" the old man asked the civil defense director.

"I'm just drawing them up now." He motioned at the nest of paper everywhere around him.

"Uh-huh! I thought so! This is an outrage! An absolute outrage! That reactor could melt tonight and you'd have no way of getting people out of this county!"

After the old man had his fill of chewing out the civil defense director I drove him back to the governor's mansion. Just as we were pulling up the governor himself came out in his shirtsleeves and took the anti-nuke's letter. About then it started to rain. Everyone ran for cover, yelling that radiation could this very minute be washing down from the sky. Before long the rain stopped but you could still see worry in their eyes.

"Maybe we should leave town," one of them yelled.

I mentioned having been implored by the anti-nuke, over

the phone, to leave town. A reporter I knew had dismissed her as a kook, I told them. But some in the crowd knew her.

"She's not a kook!" one woman answered. "She's a respected scientist!"

"What did she tell you?"

"Yes, tell us exactly what she said."

They had me repeat, word for word, the woman's message. You could see worry growing in their faces.

"If she says that maybe we should leave town," someone said.

People started leaving. I drove uneasily home through the wet streets. The house was still, Sterling asleep. I went upstairs, undressed and got into bed, not completely certain I'd wake up.

22.

In the morning there was more talk of radiation leaking from the reactor. The anti-nukes played it up for all it was worth. They'd invited a Nobel laureate into town to lecture the press. The laureate turned out to be an intense, thin little man with long gray hair covered by an absurd French beret. Reporters elbowed into the tiny meetinghall. The laureate wanted to discuss the global implications of nuclear energy. The reporters wanted to know how the radioactivity released by the reactor could be compared with a chest x-ray. The accident was far from over, he warned. He chain-smoked cigarettes and his Adam's apple bobbed as he spoke.

After the press conference I went home and called every magazine I could think of, asking to freelance a story. Nobody was interested.

Dusk gathered as I shoveled my camera and tape recorder into my pack.

"I'm going for a closer look," I told Sterling. "Maybe I can run into somebody who knows something."

"Be careful, Tom." She touched my sleeve.

The streets were deserted. It was a dark night, cloudy, and

everything shimmered with drizzle. At the little town near the reactor I got out and started walking up the main street. Not a soul in sight. In the distance I could hear laughter clapping down wet streets. It was coming from somewhere near the square.

I cut down an alley to a side street. The laughter seemed to be ringing from an old frame house in a darkened part of town. Two young men, drunk and stoned, sat on the railing of the porch. One of them, a wild-eyed kid with stringy long hair and beard, laughed maniacally. He'd stop laughing long enough to take a pull from a bottle of Jack Daniel's the other handed him. I came out of the dark, surprising them.

"What's going on?"

They were only surprised for a moment. The one resumed laughing.

"One of those stupid shit ass reporters!" he howled.

I didn't know if I should leave.

"Don't mind him," the other said. "He works at the reactor. He thinks he's been radiated to death."

The first one quit his laughing.

"A reporter are you? I want to show you something."

He stumbled inside the darkened house, motioning at me to come along. It was a dark, rundown boarding house. Not much more than a threadbare sofa and a couple of chairs littered the front room. Marijuana smoke lingered in the stale air.

The laughing one bade me to have a seat in one of the ratty chairs. He plopped himself down on the sofa, where he was joined by his buddy. They passed me the bottle of Jack. I took a pull.

"Here, have a bong," the laughing one told me. He lifted a bong and some smoke from beside the sofa.

"Jerry! He's a reporter."

"Aw shut up. Look at him. This guy gets high, don't he?" He laughed wildly.

Jerry rummaged around the sofa, lifting a Bible, waving it in my face, his eyes wild.

"We can all be dead in this house tonight!" he said.

I choked on the bong.

"Are you all right? Here man, have some water."

"We can all be dead in this house tonight!" Jerry ranted on. "We're all being radiated to death!" He started paging through the Bible, scouring the passages with wild eyes. "It's all in here!"

His friend explained that Jerry was a worker at the reactor who had become a Jehovah's Witness after the accident and who had been drinking ever since. "Here read this!" Jerry handed me a piece of paper he'd been using as a bookmark in his Bible. The paper was an official report from the electric utility stating he'd been dosed with .725 rems of gamma radiation at the reactor yesterday, nearly a quarter of his annual allowance, he said.

"Here it is in Job!" Jerry screamed. "This could be part of the prophecies. You want to know who was in the plant? The Reverend Jim Jones was in there! And people like me! Just like me!" He snatched back the paper and laughed with abandon. I wanted to leave. Making an excuse about having to be elsewhere, I got up and started backing out the door. Stumbling in the darkness, I rushed for the porch, took off at a good clip up the alley, hearing the laughter behind me, then the shout, "We can all be dead tonight! All of us! One and all!"

I jumped in my car and drove through the deserted streets, running red lights and speeding all the way back to town. I didn't give a hang about the rules of the road. Switching on the radio I heard a newsman say, "There was another series of unplanned releases from the reactor today. But plant officials said the situation is under control."

I stopped by the office for more film. Falstaff was just coming down the steps. Though we'd been feuding the events of the last few days seemed to melt much of the animosity between us.

"The anti-nukes' phone has been ringing off the hook," he said as we passed on the stairs. "It's nuts. I think some of the anti-nukes in Washington actually want a meltdown. It'd validate all the things they've been saying for years."

Back at the house Sterling was glued to the eleven o'clock news.

"They say the worst is over," she told me.

"Let's hope so. People are going crazy out there."

23.

In the morning things got crazier. The governor suddenly ordered the evacuation of pregnant women. Later we'd find out he'd wanted to order a general evacuation, but the lack of evacuation plans prevented him. So he'd hit on evacuating pregnant women, children and governors. Women and governors first. But that didn't sound right either, so he settled on the evacuation of pregnant women.

Downtown, the drunken mayor panicked and leaned on an emergency air raid siren for six minutes. You'd go to use the phone but the lines would be jammed. Fear took reprieves, then returned. One minute you'd be convinced the worst was over, then the next you'd hear something that made you want to run for your life. The nuclear plant was just so damn big you knew that if it blew there'd be a God-awful mess.

You could tell when fear had returned because the phone system would jam up. You'd pick up the phone but couldn't get a dial tone. Then, a half hour later, things would calm down enough for you to get through.

During one of these lulls when fear was in remission I got a phone call from Jenkins down at the capitol newsroom.

"I need an angle, Parker. I've decided to write about your magazine predicting a meltdown eight months before it happened."

"Remember Jenkins, the federal government almost took away our funding for publishing that article."

"Shit, Parker. This makes a nice little story now."

He said he'd file his piece the next day.

I'd just hung up the phone when a crazed anti-nuke ran into the office screaming that the government had found a hydrogen bubble in the reactor.

"Everyone's taking it as a cue to leave town! Get the hell out, while you can!"

These people weren't merely afraid of a meltdown. They had never lived through a meltdown so they had no idea what to expect. Instead they pictured the worst horror their minds could conjure, and it was this they were afraid of, ran from. Raw unbridled human fear, handed down from the darkest of our ancestral nights, the Savonarola of the bonfire of our dignities. We're afraid of ourselves.

Without drawing a breath he ran back down the steps, out of the building, hopped into his car, and was gone with a screech and a cloud of smoke.

I walked through the quiet streets to the corner lunch counter for a quick bite. Falstaff sat with some others at a table by the door.

"I always thought someday somewhere there'd be a meltdown but, you know, why'd it have to happen in my town?" He nervously laughed, pulling on a self-rolled cigarette. They were all leaving town, he said, just as soon as they'd finished eating. "It's simply, ah, too much to endure." They were all going to stay at the home of the woman who'd begged me to leave town. Suddenly she didn't seem like a kook.

I went back to the office to think things over. Outside the window it was turning into a sunny day. I walked home, skipping down the brick sidewalks with my hands shoved deep in my pockets. Sterling wasn't around. Her dogs met me at the door. I went to the phone and called a few more magazine editors.

"This reactor might blow," I told one editor. "If it does it'll be one of the biggest stories of the century. Like the wreck of the Hindenburg. And you idiots won't have anybody on the story." For all I knew, hundreds of writers were screaming the same thing at editors up and down the East Coast.

"All right, all right!" he said. "Go ahead!"

Just then Sterling came in.

"We should start thinking about what we'll do if we have to leave town," I told her. "For starters why don't we get some money out of the bank?"

"Maybe it's a good idea. I hadn't thought of it."

Other people had. We took Sterling's truck up to the bank. Long lines jammed the drive-in windows. A run on the bank.

"What're we going to do?"

"What can we do? Wait, and hope they don't run out of money."

Cars proceeded slowly past the windows. When it was our turn I emptied my account. I slipped five hundred dollars into my pocket, a thick roll of tens and twenties. It should get me through the weekend.

Back at the house I got on the phone. I couldn't find a single local politician. The phones just rang and rang. With the news of the hydrogen bubble they'd all gone with the wind. Leadership when you needed it most.

Sterling, meanwhile, made dinner. I barely had time to eat before I had to rush off down to the reactor for the eight o'clock shift change. The utility had begun using the observation center as a staging area. Bright orange school buses ferried workers to the plant.

Already it was dark and the cooling towers were all lit up

with white and blinking red lights. Behind the observation center workmen hammered together a mobile home park. You could hear drilling, the shouts of construction crews. A state cop directed traffic out front.

"What're the mobile homes for?"

"A command center. They're bringing in scientists."

My timing was good. I hadn't been standing around more than two or three minutes when a yellow school bus drove up loaded with workers at the end of their shift. I tried to be inconspicuous. Weary men with lunch pails lumbered off the bus, plodding back to their cars. When one would come by I'd quietly ask, "Excuse me," but they were mostly older workers who figured I was a reporter. They'd just walk by without saying a word. Finally a young man with bright red hair came chugging along with a goofy smile and a lunch bucket.

"Excuse me," I said softly. "Do you work in the control room?"

"Yes. I'm a technician."

"Were you working during the accident?"

"The accident was at four in the morning. I was supposed to come on at eight. When I got to work it was *crazy* in the control room. You wouldn't believe it. It was like the Twilight Zone in there. Hey, you a reporter?"

I nodded. He looked over his shoulder.

"See, I have to be careful because the company doesn't want us to talk to reporters."

Still, he seemed to want to talk. I asked for the names of the men working in the control room at the time of the accident. Talking quietly, looking over his shoulder the whole time, he gave me the names of two control room operators, the plant foreman and the shift supervisor. I took it all down on my pad, along with his phone number.

I looked at my watch. The governor had a press conference any minute. If I hurried I could just make it. Thanking the red-haired technician I flew off in my car, driving like a maniac all the way back to town, running red lights. Sloppily dressed chain-smoking paranoids crammed into the smoky pressroom in the capitol building. The same crowd as usual, only bigger. Spotting Jenkins, I joined him up front.

"Did you hear CBS is bringing in lead suits for its reporters?"

"No. I hadn't heard that."

After a long wait the governor and the lieutenant governor filed in, looking haggard and tired. The governor's shirttails hung out from the back of his pants.

"He looks scared shitless," I whispered.

"Yeah. Look how hard he's trying to hide it. That's his main job now."

The governor, his voice strained, said he'd spent the day conferring with plant officials and representatives of the federal Nuclear Regulatory Commission. He'd been assured the situation at the reactor was under control.

Several reporters, liking the sound of their own voices, kept repeating the same questions about chest and dental x-rays.

Impatient, I yelled out, "Is this a meltdown?"

A federal science advisor, looking surprised, stuttered, "We at this time don't think that's an accurate term to describe the anomaly that's occurred here."

I spotted Sterling in the back of the pressroom, slowly picking her way through the maze of cameras. To get in she'd used the press credentials I'd once given her. I made my way through the crowd to her.

"Tom, you just got a call from a magazine in New York. They're sending an editor. She'll be at the hotel downtown at midnight. They wanted to know if you could meet her there."

I looked at my watch. I still had an hour and a half.

"Mind if I have some company over?"

"What do you have in mind?"

"Maybe I'll ask this editor to stay at our house."

Sterling and I hurried home to get things ready. While we rushed around straightening things Sterling lectured, "Now don't act crazy, Tom. Try to control yourself. This editor will be looking for someone who appears to be in control of himself."

"When am I not in control of myself? Have you ever known me not to be in control of myself?"

While she lectured me the eleven o'clock news came on. The national television networks led off with the story of the governor's press conference. Suddenly there I was on national TV impatiently yelling, "Is this a meltdown?"

"You don't seem too in control of yourself there."

"I was excited. Who wouldn't be?"

A little before midnight I drove downtown to the hotel. A nice looking young woman and a neatly clipped young man stood at the curb out front. I pulled up, threw open the door.

The young woman turned out to be an assistant magazine editor. She introduced herself as Chrisandra Young. The neatly clipped young man had driven down with her from New York. He was a freelance writer named Arnold Cohen who had been assigned to cover the story for a chain of California newspapers. They hadn't checked in yet at the hotel and they jumped at the chance to stay at the house.

"Boy I'd love to interview one of the control room operators," Arnold Cohen said.

"Well I've got their names here." I held up my notepad.

Arnold Cohen's eyes bugged out.

"What a stroke of luck! I'm not in town ten minutes and already I've got the names of the control room operators!"

"Stick around. I'm just gearing up."

I suggested we go back to the house and square things away, then go down to the reactor. They followed me home in Arnold Cohen's beat-up Plymouth. When we got back to the house Sterling made something to eat. We all talked, chugging beers, while Sterling rushed around the kitchen. Arnold Cohen changed into a fresh tie and jacket.

"When you're representing a newspaper I believe you should look presentable," he told us, tying his tie in the mirror in the hallway. He was anxious to see the reactor. We all went down in my car. Even Sterling came along. I took them down to the observation center, a chaotic scene. Construction crews nailed up the command center. Scientists rushed everywhere, walking fast, looking worried. Thick cables snaked everywhichway across the ground. I watched Sterling walk through the confusion, her head almost hidden in the hood of her parka. When they'd gotten their fill of the madness we drove home through the quiet night. We put up Chrisandra Young and Arnold Cohen in the living room, on Sterling's pullout sofa.

In the morning I was the first one up. I rolled from bed, threw on some clothes, stumbled downstairs. I made so much noise I woke Arnold Cohen. He'd been sleeping with his arm around Chrisandra Young. Sitting up, he sleepily put on his glasses.

"Where do you get your energy?"

"I want to see if we can talk to these control room operators."

We got a little something to eat then went over to the office. Chrisandra Young and Arnold Cohen took in the place, studying the layers of faded paper on the bulletin board.

"Why don't you clean off this board?" Chrisandra Young picked at the flyers. "Here's a notice for a George McGovern pot luck."

"Don't touch that bulletin board. It's bad luck."

Two of the control room operators and one shift supervisor were listed in the phone book. I dialed a number. A drunk man picked up.

"Why don't you reporters leave town?" he slurred at me. "You're really making more of this than it is."

"He's got one of them on the phone."

Arnold Cohen picked up the extension. He tried to get the guy to say more. The man only hung up, with a loud slam of the phone.

"Well how do you like that?"

"He sounded absolutely crocked, didn't he?"

None of the other reactor operators answered their phones. We decided to visit them at home.

"We should split up then."

Chrisandra Young came with me, Arnold Cohen took his own car. For an hour and a half we drove all around the countryside. None of the control room operators were home. "Maybe Arnold is having more luck," Chrisandra Young said. "He's a pretty good reporter." She wanted to see the sports arena where evacuated families camped out on the floor of an ice hockey rink. We drove over, walked among the evacuees and cots and cardboard boxes filled with emergency supplies, stopping occasionally to snap pictures.

Chrisandra excused herself to call her boss in New York. For several minutes I walked around the arena. I was so filled with what was happening around me that I realized I couldn't remember what Chrisandra Young looked like. At last I spotted her, walking among the refugees. She had high cheek bones and wavy hair that fell around her shoulders.

"New York's pleased with the way things are going," she said, walking up. I was glad New York was glad. "They've assigned another writer to the story. We're supposed to keep an eye out for him."

"Another writer?"

"A movie writer from Hollywood."

"Hollywood? A movie writer?"

"They want him for his name. It's a coup that they got him. A real coup in the publishing world. Don't worry. We'll work it all out later."

The electric utility's executives called a press conference at a nearby VFW. We were supposed to meet Arnold Cohen there. It only took a few minutes to drive over. When we arrived the place was already crammed with reporters. Inside, at the podium up front, two utility executives combatively asserted that the situation at the reactor was under control. One of them was the utility president who, months earlier, had told me there'd never be a meltdown at *his* nuclear plant. Now there must have been a hundred microphones stuck to the podium in front of him. The snarling utility executives had to stand on milk boxes to be seen above the bristle of microphones. From atop the boxes they snarled and tore at the air like tamed lions.

"I don't see why we have to tell you every little thing we do," one of them roared into the din. It was the same executive who'd helicoptered to the observation center on the day of the accident, the one who'd said everything was under control. Just a little water spilled on the floor.

"Look at him. He's wearing the same blue suit he wore three days ago. It must be the only suit he has."

"I thought something about this smelled."

We found Arnold Cohen in front of the speaker's podium. He also had no luck tracking down the control room operators. He had, however, run into New York columnist Jimmy Breslin. He laughed that Breslin had gone into the toilet, only to emerge complaining of radiation. "'Hey, it came off in my hand!'"

Arnold Cohen took in the crowd.

"Would you look at all these reporters!" he went on. "I covered Watergate, and there weren't as many reporters covering the fall of a president as there are covering this."

We were hungry. I suggested a McDonald's down the road.

"McDonald's? Can't we go someplace better than that?"

"I'm not thinking of the food. I'm thinking of the story. I'm wondering what the mood is like there. People all over the country will be able to identify with a McDonald's."

"That sounds logical."

Tensions in fact ran high beneath the golden arches. People sat at the plastic tables wearing dosimeters in their lapels, talking excitedly about the latest news flashes. A waitress dropped a stack of trays and a young girl shrieked, "I don't want to die!" Others laughed.

Afterward we drove back to the house. Sterling had decided to leave town. She rushed around the house gathering things up.

"There's talk of a meltdown," she said. She was stuffing the dogs' dishes into a bag. "I don't trust the utility *or* the government. Those fuckers have been lying to us all along."

While Sterling dashed about I turned on the TV. The network news came on. The anchorman said a meltdown might be imminent. Behind the anchorman flashed a copy of our magazine. They told how we'd predicted a meltdown eight months earlier. The network reporter finished his story standing in front of the welcome sign at the edge of town. At the bottom of the sign, for millions of eyes to behold, were the hurriedly scrawled words "Nex is Sex."

24.

"Now this is exciting!" Sterling said.

I numbly stood by the TV, a beer in hand.

The phone started ringing. Friends called asking what was going on. Nate Freeman called from Seattle, wondering when I'd leave town. "You're not chasing a posthumous Pulitzer, are you?"

"No. I'm chasing something else." I looked at Sterling.

My friends Tony and Beth called to say they were evacuating to South Carolina. If things got bad I could stay in their cabin in the mountains.

"Didn't I tell you that movie gave me the creeps?" Tony asked.

"It's been like this the whole time you were out," Sterling said between calls. "Your friends John and Mike called asking when you were leaving. Maybe it's time you started thinking about leaving, Tom."

"It might be a good idea to start making plans at that," Chrisandra Young said. She managed to find a break between incoming calls to phone her boss. "Good news!" she announced, hanging up. "I'm authorized to arrange for hotel rooms for all of us far out in the country."

"Whoopee!" Arnold Cohen swigged a beer. "Now we're on a big-time expense account! Sterling, you can come with us to the hotel."

She pursed her lips, shook her head no.

"I'm going home. My parents will be upset if I don't get out of here. They've been calling all day."

Sterling asked me to help her carry some things down from her room. I followed her up. She closed the door after me.

"Promise me you'll leave town," she said.

"Sure."

I helped carry down her skis. Why she needed them at the end of March in a meltdown I'll never know. She said she might never be able to return for them. She looked around at all the things she couldn't take with her on short notice. "Things," she said. "What do I care?" Events were catching up with her.

"I just this minute realized I might never see this place again," she said, looking around.

I helped her take her dogs out to the truck. She loaded them into the back, waved good-bye, and was gone.

I went inside. Chrisandra Young quietly picked my guitar in the kitchen.

"So you play guitar too," I said.

"When I first came to New York it's how I earned my living. Playing in clubs."

She sang a short song, her fingers dancing across the fretboard. She had a pleasant voice.

People kept phoning to say they were leaving town. Jim Robbins, a friend from the magazine, asked me over for one last beer. He lived just a few blocks away. Excusing myself, I walked down the back alleys, over the cracked brick sidewalks. Robbins seemed sad, thoughtful. He was a tall, moustached man with a perpetual nervous twitch in his eyes.

"You know the government might never let us back," he

said, his eyes twitching. "I've heard it might be years before they start letting us back in, and only then in protective lead suits to get some of our things."

We raised our beers and drank a toast to the stinking old town.

"You know you should probably think about leaving too, Tom. No use taking unnecessary chances."

"Sure. No use in that."

By the time I got back to the house Chrisandra Young had just stepped out of the shower. Wrapped in a robe, she dried her hair with a towel.

"What's on your agenda for tonight, Tom?"

"Oh I thought we'd make the rounds."

Arnold Cohen wanted to stay home. The newspaper chain in California wanted him to submit copy for tomorrow's bulldog. He only had a little portable so I let him use my Selectric.

Chrisandra Young and I took off in my car, heading downtown. A lot of people had left. It was the deadest Saturday night I'd ever seen. None of the kids cruised the circuit. Nobody walked along the river, which looked quiet, red and lonely.

"Now tonight," I told Chrisandra Young, driving like a madman down Front Street, "we'll see what this stinking town is all about. Normally it's a pretty dead place but tonight it's the last place on earth any sane person would want to be."

I hung a hard left on Market Street. Much to my surprise Market Square was all lit up. People bustled everywhere. Usually downtown was dead on a Saturday night. Now smartly dressed people walked about windowshopping the sad storefronts. They were out-of-towners in for the meltdown. We parked, got out, walked around. A carnival atmosphere. No panic at all. People displayed the same sort of confidence that must have visited those in the Titanic's dance band. Couples walked gaily by, arm in arm, everyone nodding hello to each other. Some were drunk, dressed in bright colors, laughing, talking to each other. They all half expected to die.

"People sure are friendly tonight," I heard Chrisandra Young say.

"They've decided to stay for the duration."

We were in a dreamy haze. We stumbled wide-eyed around the square, stopping to chat idly with strangers. The discussions invariably centered, with a laugh, on whether it would blow or blow over.

Chrisandra Young followed me to the county courthouse. An old woman stopped me at the door. She placed her hand on mine.

"You're so young," she said. "Don't you have relatives you can stay with out of town?"

I asked the same of her.

"Oh my Lord young fella," she laughed, showing broken teeth. "I was born in this town and I'm going to die in this town. If the good Lord says that should happen tonight who am I to say otherwise?"

We went into the courthouse. People ran everywhere. You would have thought it was noon Monday.

All this activity mystified Chrisandra Young.

"We love disasters in this town," I tried to explain. "You should have seen it last time the river flooded. Everyone came out to help. Catastrophes give us an excuse to be nice to each other."

In the basement of the courthouse, in a narrow hallway leading to the emergency preparedness office, radiation survival kits lay in boxes on the floor, free for the taking. The boxes held Geiger counters, first aid supplies, copies of Life Magazine from the early sixties detailing what to do in the event of nuclear holocaust. We used to fear the Russians.

An elderly volunteer told us the director of county civil defense was locked away somewhere drawing up evacuation plans. His wife seemed to be running things in the office. She spoke calmly to the people who wandered in to help. Here the civil defense director had no evacuation plans but strangers showed up off the street to help.

We returned to the street to look for a cup of coffee. Only one restaurant in the whole town was open, it seemed. All the other restauranteurs had fled. It was a small greasy spoon on the town square, doing a booming business with out-of-town reporters. Coffee at five dollars a cup. A sign in the window said there was a one-minute limit on seats inside.

"Let's not buy anything from this gouger." We walked back to the car without coffee.

I told her as we drove off into the night, "Tonight this town's the last place on earth anyone would want to be. This stinking little town has finally de-evolved into the last place on earth."

We barreled down the deserted streets, passing the sad Oddfellow's Home.

"Now here, this must be the *absolute* last place on earth! Those poor old oddfellows. I wonder if they've been evacuated?"

Spinning around, I swung into the long dark driveway leading up to the grand front entrance of the old mansion. We tried the front door but it was locked.

"They must have been evacuated," Chrisandra Young said. We stood wordlessly in the darkness, looking at each other. It put things in perspective. They'd gotten rid of the oddfellows yet I was still stuck at the last place on earth.

Staggering off the porch, I walked out into the grass. I looked up at the few stars I could see shining between the slow-moving, murky clouds. I found myself thinking about Sterling, even worrying about whether her dogs were safe. Here I was caught up in the excitement of being with an attractive, big-city reporter, and I couldn't shake these sad thoughts of my roommate with the funny mouth movements.

"Is something wrong, Tom?"

I smiled.

"No. I was just thinking about the river. I used to swim in it as a boy. And the old brick sidewalks in front of my office. I might never walk on those bricks again. They're red, the color of rust. Most every one is cracked. I never realized what that old brick sidewalk meant to me."

"A moment ago you were saying it was a stinking little town and now you're moaning about the brick sidewalks?"

"I'm a pile of contradictions, aren't I?"

"Oh yes you're so complex."

I pulled myself together and we drove down to the reactor. The observation center was a madhouse of scientists and nuclear technicians. It was a full-blown emergency. Dozens of mobile homes had been set up for the scientists. Everybody rushed around looking worried.

I recognized one of the plant workers. I'd first seen him on the day of the accident. He'd been one of the workers sitting at the picnic tables watching the reactor. Then they'd laughed at me because I didn't know how the reactor worked. Now one of them paced around the grounds of the observation center in his pajamas and robe. Recognizing me, he came over and started apologizing for the way his co-workers had treated me the day of the accident.

"I didn't think it was right the way they made fun of you." He had a sincere face. "I just wanted you to know that I think they were wrong to make fun of you the way they did." Behind him lights on the cooling towers were blinking. "Maybe we should have tried to explain this thing better."

The reactor, he said, had been his life. He'd worked there ever since it'd been built. Tonight he was out at the observation center in his pajamas and robe because he couldn't sleep, he said. Listening to the news at home alarmed him. He'd come to see if things were under control. He felt reassured watching all the scientists running around.

"These are some of the greatest minds in the world," he said. He lifted his hand at the mobile home park. "They're going to work this problem out. I know they will."

Down by the road reporters looked out over the river at the reactor and the tall cooling towers. A wild-eyed writer sputtered it was going to blow. He was covering the disaster for a string of magazines, he said. He stood beside a four-wheel-drive pickup with a small jury-rigged satellite dish on the cab. When we came upon him he was gazing out over the water through a pair of binoculars, a can of beer in hand. Would we like a beer? he asked. "Sounds great." Digging around in the back of his truck, he pulled two cold Buds from a small refrigerator.

"It's going to pop just like a champagne cork," he said. He flicked his thumb at the dome across the water. He laughed, winking. "Steam explosion. But do you know what? I'm not worried. Do I look like a worried man? This is the safest place on earth to be. Right here. You bet your ass on that. Believe me, I have. I've figured it out. From here we'll be able to see which way the wind's blowing. I'm just going to hop in my truck and drive as fast as I can in the opposite direction. I've got a weather vane on top of my truck there, you see." He pointed to a tiny wind indicator spinning on the cab of his truck, beside the satellite dish. "When I get fifty kilometers away I'm going to stop the truck just long enough to aim that dish at a weather satellite, patch in with my computer" (we saw he had a small computer in his pickup) "and I'll get the long-range prognosis. From there, who knows? I can take this thing up into the mountains. Hell, I can be in Chicago by morning. Want to see something else?" He patted his stomach. A dull thud rose from beneath his shirt. He drew up his shirttail, exposing a patch of gray. "Lead underwear," he winked. Again he loudly slapped his lead belly.

He was prepared, all right. He had a radio and he kept sweeping the airwaves for clues. But all he got was the taped chatter of a primitive people.

"Saturday! Saturday! See Big Wheels crush nineteen four-by-fours in a flash of thunder and lightning. See nitro-burning funny cars. Saturday! Saturday! Golden Grove Speedway. Be there!"

"I'll bet he'll be disappointed if it doesn't blow," I said to Chrisandra Young as we walked away.

"You're getting your humor back, Tom. I was afraid you were cracking up back there. The way you were going on about the river and the bricks in your sidewalks."

Walking a short distance down the river, we looked out over the slow-moving water at the gnarl of pipes and buildings, cooling towers and blinking lights. We hadn't walked far when along hurried this wiry, pale looking fellow. He introduced himself as a wire service reporter.

"Do you know that UPI has just reported the government is going to try to burst the hydrogen bubble?"

He said this calmly, so as not to instill undue panic.

"No," I said. "We hadn't heard that."

"It's just come over the wire. These scientists are like babes playing in the woods."

The three of us looked at each other.

"Well," I said to the wire service reporter, "maybe it's time we moseyed along."

"And which direction do you think you'll be moseying in?"

"Oh, I don't know." I wet my thumb and stuck it in the breeze. The wind was coming from the north. "We'll probably be moseying north."

"Yes, that does seems to me to be a very good direction to mosey in. I'll think I'll probably mosey north myself."

With that he took off at a fair clip for his car, hopped in, spun around and moseyed off at about eighty-five miles an hour. It was just a Ford sedan but he made that baby rip, flashing over the hill in a rattle of tire smoke and exhaust.

Chrisandra Young turned to me.

"Do you get the feeling these scientists don't know what they're doing?"

"Yes, the same thought crossed my mind."

I had the presence of mind to drop a dime into the pay phone out in front of the observation center. I called home. My father answered.

"These scientists don't know what they're doing," I told him. "You better get out of town."

There was a pause.

"And you? Are you leaving too?"

"Yes. I'll be leaving too."

I returned to the roadside. As I came walking up a crazed man, bolstered by drink, charged the main gate and tried to climb over the fence.

"Only I can solve this mess!" he bellowed, rattling up the fence.

Guards jumped all over him. While we watched they carted him off. All the while he yelled out the back of the paddy wagon that everyone would die, our time had come.

"I'm starting to wonder if this was such a choice assignment," Chrisandra Young said.

"It's not going to blow," we heard someone say. It'd come from a tall scientist standing nearby. He was watching the reactor from the riverside. A toothpick poked from his mouth. He stood calmly chewing the toothpick, watching the reactor, the calmest man you'd ever want to see. He looked a little like Robert Redford. "They're going to get control of her. She's coming around now. Wait and see."

His calm bearing and the fact that he vaguely resembled Robert Redford worked like a soothing balm on us. One of the reasons I'd been feeling uneasy about things was that there were no heroes in any of the scenes, no good-looking leading men like you'd see in a Hollywood movie. Only short dumpy excited fellows, the yahoos of my hometown, running around screaming their fool heads off. Now that we'd run into someone who looked vaguely like Robert Redford we straightaway started feeling better about things.

"I could use another beer," I said to Chrisandra Young.

"So could I."

We drove to a bar a little way down the road. It was packed with plant workers and reporters. Everyone was getting plastered. "I'm not worried about radiation," one pot-bellied nuclear worker yelled across the ruckus at us. "If you drink enough beer it'll wash right out of you."

We started to drink pretty hard. Chrisandra Young became engaged in conversation with a tall and lean reporter who wore a cowboy hat. She stood beside the cowboy with a beer in hand, swinging her lithe body from a support pole. I thought the cowboy was going to pick her up but before long she brushed him off.

We didn't evacuate that night. I took Chrisandra Young back to the house. When we came in Arnold Cohen was already asleep in the sofa bed.

"Do you want to sleep in a waterbed?"

Chrisandra Young nodded her head.

We quietly went up the steps. I took her into Sterling's room. It was dark and the room was still. I pulled back the covers. The waterbed quivered under the blanket.

"At least you should be more comfortable here than on the sofa bed," I told her.

She put her knee on the bed.

"What about you? You don't want to sleep here tonight?"

I shook my head no.

We said goodnight. I went down the hall to the guest room and closed the door.

25.

Sometime around two or three in the morning the phone rang.
"So you didn't leave?" It was Sterling.
"Where are you?"
"At my mom's house. Answer my question. You promised you'd leave town."
"Why should I?"
"Tom, are you trying to kill yourself?"
"What's it to you?"
"I do care about you, you know."
"Yeah I hear you."
"I'm coming down there first thing in the morning. We'll talk about it then, okay?"
"Sure."

26.

I didn't sleep too well that night. Mostly I laid awake. The walls seemed too thin to provide any real protection. In the morning I went out to get the papers. I came quietly down the steps but still I woke Arnold Cohen, sleeping alone on the sofa bed.
"Where *do* you get your energy?" he asked again. His eyes were heavy with early-morning drowsiness. I hurried over to the drug store, bought as many newspapers as I could find. Jenkins' story ran in all of them.
When I got back to the house we read the papers and drank coffee at the table.
"Look. Says here the president is coming to town today."
"The president? That figures. First they drop the bomb then the president says a few words."
"Wonder how they'll try to whitewash this over."
Sterling came in.
"Hello," Arnold Cohen said. "I thought you'd evacuated."
"I came back for a few things." Sterling looked at me. "Tom, would you mind giving me a hand upstairs?"
I followed Sterling up to her room. She took in her unmade waterbed.

"I let Chrisandra Young sleep on your bed last night. I didn't think you'd mind."

Sterling closed the door.

"Tom, let's leave town."

"Just like that? I've an assignment with a national magazine. Remember? I've a few little things to cover, like the arrival of the president of the United States."

"I don't give a damn about the president. He's not worth dying for, is he?"

I wondered if her fright was driving her crazy, or bringing her real emotions finally to the surface.

"You've treated me like a sack of potatoes all these months and now that I'm finally making something of myself you expect me to pull out at the snap of your fingers. Remember when you said you wanted to go ice camping? I couldn't get you to do it if my life depended on it. All these months that tent of yours has sat down there on the floor by the door."

"Do you want to go camping, Tom? Is that it? We'll take the tent and leave right away."

"We'll talk about it later. Now I've got a job to do."

Chrisandra Young, Arnold Cohen and I drove down to the reactor to see the president. We took my car. Unfortunately Chrisandra Young and Arnold Cohen had no press credentials and couldn't get in. They let me into the meetinghall but suddenly I was swamped by Secret Service agents who wanted a look at my Boy Scout yucca pack. They rummaged around my pack, finding only my tape recorder and camera.

"You ought to get your magazine to buy you a briefcase," one of the agents said.

The meetinghall swarmed with reporters. Photographers squirmed for a place up front. I was early and found a place in the first row. Late arrivals tried to gyp.

"I've been waiting here a gaddamn hour and I'll be gaddamned if you're going to set up in front of me!" one reporter yelled at a camera crew that tried to gyp in.

"All right, all right, we're going."

"How do you like that! The nerve of some people! Animals!"

The president came out with the governor. He said he knew-ah if the areah had to be-ah evacuated everyone would, ah, remain calm. With that he turned and hurriedly left the building, his big motorcade racing away, sirens screaming. Hardly the Gettysburg Address, hardly worth the wait. I despondently went back outside. Chrisandra Young and Arnold Cohen waited at the curb.

"How'd it go?"

"It was a splendid speech."

"The writer from Hollywood's finally shown up," Chrisandra Young said.

"It's safe enough for the president so he probably figures it's safe enough for him," Arnold Cohen added.

I should have seen it coming. Now that the president had shown up, uttered a few words and headed for the hills, there was only one thing more preposterous that could happen.

Hollywood had shown up in a rented Lincoln Continental towne car. White. Red crushed velour seats. Hollywood wore an Australian bushman's hat, a gold chain around the neck, a silk shirt open halfway down the hairy chest.

The writer from Hollywood hit his horn. He waved. He smiled.

We walked across the street to the shiny Lincoln. Two men sat in the car. The one behind the wheel stuck out his hand, introducing himself as Rex Redux, Hollywood screenwriter extraordinaire. With him, in the passenger's seat, was his personal photographer, Lance Cullpepper. Both had come in time for the presidential press conference. Lacking press credentials, they couldn't get in.

Hollywood bade us to climb inside the Lincoln towne car so

we could go eat lunch, see the reactor. Chrisandra Young, Arnold Cohen and I got into the backseat. That red crushed velour really made you sink in deep.

27.

So there I was, in the backseat of a gold-plated pimpmobile with a New York magazine editor and a screenwriter from Hollywood.

"Where have you been?" Chrisandra Young asked the movie writer. "We were beginning to think you weren't going to show."

"We were delayed in Chicago." Rex Redux explained he was experiencing trouble financing his sojourn into journalism. "This damn Lincoln is costing me a fortune to rent. Do you have my advance check? My agent *did* tell you I want half my fee up front, didn't he?"

"I'll call New York and find out about it as soon as I can get to a phone."

"Good. Things seem to be going well," said Rex Redux. "Now if only I can find someone who can tell me what happened at the reactor."

We told him we already had the names of the control room operators. I said I had a source who was inside the control room the morning of the accident.

"Tremendous!" Rex Redux clapped his hands together.

"The whole way in we were wondering how we'd get the names of the control room operators. Didn't know what I was going to do. Thought maybe I'd have to go to the utility and try taking a receptionist out to lunch or something. Thought maybe I could try stealing the names off her Rolodex. I didn't know."

We passed the gates of the reactor. Pandemonium. Tractor trailers were hauling in what looked like huge reinforced concrete barriers. The big concrete slabs almost made Rex Redux choke.

"Would you look at that!" he yelled. "Blast shields! They're bringing in blast shields! They're expecting it to blow! What in God's name am I doing here?"

We drove to the observation center and split up, hoping to find someone willing to talk. It was a little after noon and the shifts were changing. I spotted the red-haired technician coming my way.

"It's you again," he said, walking up. He invited me over to his apartment.

I ran through the crowd to tell the others. When I found Chrisandra Young she said, "Arnold just found someone who's willing to talk." She pointed to Arnold Cohen and Rex Redux. They were just waving good-bye to the same red-haired technician I'd been talking with, saying they'd see him later. The red-haired technician looked all star-struck at having met a Hollywood movie writer.

"That's my source, Chrisandra. He's invited us over to his apartment."

Rex Redux came over. Before he did one more thing, he said, he had to eat lunch. He asked if I knew a good place to eat. Piling back into the Lincoln, I had them take the back roads. When we got to the restaurant Chrisandra Young excused herself to call her boss.

She came back.

"Rex, your advance check should arrive tomorrow."

"Good." The screenwriter dug zestfully into his lunch. "Things are going just marvelously, aren't they? I couldn't have hoped any better. Not in town an hour, and already I have the names of the control room operators. I've set up an interview. You know what?" He looked at me. "I have a good mind to give you a little credit line at the bottom of my story. You know, something like, thanks for the help of so and so."

"*Your* story?" I choked on my sandwich. "I have a good mind to give you a little credit line at the bottom of *my* story."

"Take it easy, Tom," Chrisandra Young said. "We'll straighten all this out, I'm sure."

We finished eating and drove back to get my car. Out of the blue Arnold Cohen suggested Chrisandra Young and I not go along to interview the red-haired technician. Chrisandra Young had to catch a train to New York.

"Why don't you take her to the station?" Cohen said to me.

I had to shout at someone. I didn't especially want to blow up at Chrisandra Young. I didn't especially want to blow up at the movie writer from Hollywood. That left Arnold Cohen.

"You asshole, Cohen. What the hell are you doing here, anyway?"

Arnold Cohen looked surprised.

"You just can't blow in here and steal my sources."

"Now listen kid, take it easy," Rex Redux said. "I'd prefer it myself if you didn't come along. Your instincts are an unknown quantity."

"My instincts have gotten me this far. And my instincts tell me to go along on this interview."

"Listen, Arnold and I'll go interview this kid then we'll meet up with you and I'll personally tell you everything he says. I promise. I'll personally see to it that nobody fucks you over." Rex Redux gave me a wink.

"What's the matter with you, Tom?" Chrisandra Young

asked. "You were fine until a few minutes ago. Until back at the restaurant. Then you got all weird."

"Maybe it has something to do with standing in front of that reactor for your magazine all these days."

I was about ready to kiss them all off. I told myself I'd go to the red-haired technician's apartment in my own car, if that's what I had to do, and sell the interview somewhere else. I reached to my back pocket for my notepad. It was gone! I knew I couldn't say anything about it. They'd say I was inexperienced for sure if I told them I'd lost my notes. Without saying a word I searched around the backseat of the Lincoln. No luck. Had Arnold Cohen, hoping to get me out of the way, taken my notes back at the restaurant? In a stunning about-face I told Chrisandra Young I'd take her to the train.

"Now you're seeing reason," she said. "Don't worry, Tom. Nobody's going to fuck you over. I've got *power* at the magazine."

I drove Chrisandra Young down to the train station. On the way we passed a crowd of Catholics in front of a church. The bishop stood before the crowd, swinging an incense burner over kneeling supplicants, granting everyone general absolution. It was another case of being in the right place at the right time. We passed the big welcome sign on the way into town. An old man was up on the billboard whitewashing over the words "Nex is Sex."

At the train station's snack counter, over coffee, Chrisandra Young told the waitress she should think about leaving town. The waitress threw her wash rag to the counter.

"Look, if you're afraid *you* get out. I'm staying. If it melts, I'll melt with it."

Out in the station people hurried by with luggage. They announced Chrisandra Young's train. She gave me a hug.

"Take care of yourself, Tom. You were a good person to spend a catastrophe with."

The instant she boarded her train I raced back to the restaurant. I found my notepad on the counter by the cash register. It was too late for the interview, but at least I'd found my notes.

I had a couple of hours to kill so I went back to the office. I was sorting through the mail when Lenny Popadopolis, the spontaneous human combustion expert, came in.

"Now we're in for it!" he yelled. "The FBI is investigating us!"

He threw a copy of his eight-month-old meltdown article down in front of me, along with several newspaper clippings.

"They think we sabotaged the reactor!"

We'd been victimized by yet another amazing coincidence. The reactor had melted on its first birthday, March 28, one year to the day after its first nuclear chain reaction on March 28 the year before. In his prediction article Lenny Popadopolis wrote, "ever since the reactor became radioactive on March 28, the utility had been having trouble with it." Some wire service reporter, hurriedly reading a copy of the magazine that we'd passed out on the day of the accident, misconstrued the words "became radioactive" to mean "melted." It'd gone out over the wire that not only had Lenny Popadopolis predicted the meltdown eight months before it happened, the nuclear Nostradamus had predicted the *exact day* it would melt. Some right-wing fundamentalist Christian in North Carolina had read the wire service report and immediately began writing letters to major newspapers, demanding the FBI investigate us.

I was speechless.

Speaking of himself in his customary plural form, Lenny Popadopolis began whining, "We're sorry you talked us into writing about a complete meltdown. We would have been happy to write about just a little water spilled on the floor."

"Don't worry. We've got a good attorney. We'll go downtown to see him tomorrow. Should I pick you up or do you have a car?"

"No, we'll need a ride."

"*We'll* need a ride?"

"Our car's in the shop."

"Look, Lenny, when you say we'll need a ride do you mean *you'll* need a ride. Just yourself? Or are you saying you'll be bringing someone with you? If only for practical reasons could you please let me know? I might only have one seat in my car."

"We mean, we'll be coming with just ourselves. But we might have to evacuate tonight if the reactor melts. Do you mind if we consult our psychic?"

"By all means, go ahead."

He picked up the phone and called some psychic in Chicago, asking if it would be safe for him to remain in town overnight. He held the phone for a few minutes while she went off to consult her Ouija board or her tarot cards or the stars or entrails or God only knows what. Then she came back on. Thanking her gratefully, he hung up the phone.

"Good news," he told me. "Our psychic says the meltdown is over. We can sleep safe and sound in our own bed tonight."

"Funny," I said, "earlier today I saw the president of the United States. He seemed to be under the impression there might be an explosion."

"No," Lenny Popadopolis said. He calmly shook his head. "The meltdown's over."

Feeling better about things, the spring back in his step, Lenny Popadopolis turned to leave.

"Wait a minute."

"Yes?"

"Tell me. Why do you always refer to yourself in the plural?"

"Didn't you ever have the feeling there's more than one entity in your head?"

"No. Can't say I have."

No sooner had he left than I got a phone call from a reporter with a Philadelphia newspaper.

"What're you boys up to?" I asked.

In fact I knew what they were up to, had been reading about it for a few days. The desperate electric utility had flown in a big-city public relations team, billeting the PR specialists in a local hotel. The Philadelphia paper wasted no time stationing several reporters outside the spin doctors' hotel room. The reporters listened through the keyhole. They shamelessly reported they'd overheard the PR practitioners saying things like, "We've got to put a positive spin on this! Tell the public something like, 'This, ah, incident only proves the damn things just won't, well, blow up!'"

They say in the great Johnstown flood people were warned of the impending disaster but, not knowing the messenger, they didn't run. In the curious case of this nuclear inundation, despite numerous reassurances from scientists, the government, and the utility that the reactor wouldn't blow, all reported by keyhole-peeping newspapermen, people ran for their lives. The public knew all the messengers, trusted only their feet.

Now, on the phone, the reporter from the Philadelphia paper said he'd heard it through the grapevine I had the names of several reactor control room operators. Probably through Jenkins. He said his paper had resorted to stationing several reporters at the main gate of the reactor. Their job was to write down hundreds of license plate numbers of cars leaving the plant. They'd send someone down to the state Department of Transportation to pay five or ten bucks apiece to trace the licenses. But still they hadn't come up with the names of the control room operators. Could they buy some information from me? the reporter wanted to know. I said I wasn't interested in selling information. Perhaps I'd consider writing a by-lined article for them, I said. Great, he said. How much money did I want?

The magazine's printing bill was due.

"How about six hundred dollars?"

"Hey, no problem. We'll send someone by later with a check."

I gave him the name of a control room operator.

I'd just put down the phone when I got a call from a reporter with the Washington Post. He wanted to interview me about Lenny Popadopolis' meltdown prediction. I told the story, how the government had revoked our funding, throwing in how I'd just been offered cash by the Philadelphia paper.

"How much did they offer?"

"Six hundred."

"Is that all?"

"All I really want is the by-line."

He said he'd check with his editor. Five minutes didn't go when he called back saying the Post was interested. A reporter would come around later that day to talk.

It was turning out to be a good day for business.

I tripped out of the office and danced down the brick sidewalks home. Sterling wasn't around. The phone rang and rang. The caller was with a West German magazine. In halting English he explained he and a colleague were in town for the meltdown. He'd read about our meltdown prediction and said it was important that he see me. I tried to beg off. He was insistent. Finally I broke down.

Before long I heard a knock. In came two German magazine writers. Blond. Blue eyed. Lugging cameras and tape recorders.

We sat down at the kitchen table. One of them, a compact man with a piercing look, offered me a European cigarette.

"Vould you like?"

"No thanks. I don't smoke."

They both took a smoke, slowly lighting them. They held them off to the side, the pungent brown smoke curling slowly around their heads.

"This is a terrible thing, this reactor mishap, isn't it?" the one with the piercing look said.

"There hasn't been as much excitement around here since Robert E. Lee went shopping for shoes in Gettysburg."

He gave me an odd look.

"This is quite a setback to the vorldvide nuclear establishment, vouldn't you say? That is, there must be some people who are quite happy about it, no?"

"How do you mean?"

He laughed coyly. So did his partner.

"People whose ends it might serve."

"I'm not sure I follow."

Again they laughed coyly.

"You don't have to be afraid of us."

The other nodded.

"I don't really know what you're talking about."

"In Europe ve have groups, revolutionaries some vould call them, such as Baader-Meinhof."

"The Red Brigades," the other threw in.

"Yes. The Red Brigades. Groups who, for a lack of a better word, sabotage military industrial installations."

"And you think that's what happened here?"

Taking out a copy of The New York Times, he pointed to a paragraph describing how our magazine had predicted not only the meltdown but the *exact day* the meltdown would occur.

"Don't be afraid of us," the first one repeated. "Ve have a theory. Ve thought perhaps you might put us in contact with the revolutionary group responsible for this, hm, mishap."

For a few seconds I did nothing but look at them. They did nothing but look at me. The smoke curled around their heads from those spicy cigarettes they held out at the sides of the faces.

I broke into mad laughter.

They laughed too.

"You think there's a Baader-Meinhof gang around here?"

"Might it be possible?"

"Only if the terror squad was run by the Katzenjammer Kids."

"You vould have to admit that this is a remarkable coincidence," the second one said, tapping the newspaper.

"So you two think my magazine had something to do with this?" I laughed again.

They too laughed, shaking their heads yes.

I tried to explain to them how I'd had the expert in spontaneous human combustion write the meltdown prediction, about the unfortunate copy editing oversight involving the dates, but I could see they didn't believe a word of it. It all did sound preposterous. I told them I was a writer, like they were, not a terrorist. To prove my claim I offered to sell them a piece of writing.

"You have some vriting you vould like to sell to our magazine?"

"Yes. Would you like to see it?"

"Yes, by all means, yes."

I ran upstairs, fetching an article I'd written several months earlier, one describing how the electric utility had tried to take our federal funding away. The two sat at the table reading with interest.

"And how much vould you normally ask for a piece of vriting like this?"

"Oh, I don't know. How about a hundred and fifty dollars?"

They looked at each other, nodding in agreement.

They bought the article on the spot. It was the easiest damn sale I'd ever made.

Thanking me repeatedly for my time, they gave me their cards showing where they could be reached in Germany if I decided to loosen up and tell them about the terrorists. Oversized, European business cards.

"Do not be afraid of us," the first one said again, winking. Just as they were leaving Sterling came in.

One of them bowed, kissing her hand. He looked at her significantly, like she was Mata Hari. Looking in my direction once more, he went out the door with his companion.

28.

Not long after that the door opened and in came Arnold Cohen, Rex Redux and his personal photographer, Lance Cullpepper. I didn't have to introduce the last two to Sterling, as Cullpepper had already pulled a glossy movie industry broadside from his camera bag. Pointing to their names printed on the slick-paper sheet, he said, "We worked with Jane Fonda."

Sterling didn't care. They couldn't comprehend we might be more concerned about our town blowing up than we were about Jane Fonda.

The meeting with the red-haired control room worker had gone well. Rex Redux paced happily around the room, rubbing his hands together. Having been in town only for the afternoon he'd gotten completely to the bottom of the whole affair. True to his promise, he drew a diagram of the reactor on a paper napkin, explaining to me in detail what had gone wrong. In the best Hollywood fashion he used his hands to dramatize the size of the reactor and what he called "the cataclysmic forces" behind the accident.

"You have no idea how *mammoth* things are over in that reactor building, the *colossal* size of everything, the *Herculean* forces those workers must combat every day of their lives." You would have thought he'd just written a script and was trying to sell it to a producer.

Rex Redux said he thought chances were still good the reactor might blow. Better than fifty fifty. Not good odds. Not good at all. He worried out loud about staying in the hotel downtown. Just twelve miles from the reactor. He didn't know. He didn't know at all. Maybe we should find a place far out in the mountains where we all could stay, just in case, he said. I promised I'd meet up with him at the hotel in a few hours. We'd work something out then, I promised. The three of them left.

"What rock did they crawl out from under?" Sterling wanted to know.

Now I had only to wait for the reporter from the Washington Post. It was dark before I heard the knock. He looked just like a young Jimmy Stewart. His hair was neat and short. He wore an expensive camel overcoat. He seemed surprised by my scruffy appearance. We suspiciously eyed each other, almost circling. We were from two different worlds, I saw. The movie of his life and the movie of my life met at this strange crossroads.

I gave him the names of the control room operators and their phone numbers. I briefly explained to him, with the help of Rex Redux's napkin, what had happened inside the reactor. The whole time he stood there bobbing his head, taking it all in. "Uh-huh. Yeah, I follow. Uh-huh." He even sounded like Jimmy Stewart. "Yah, yah," he said, "We'll be in touch. Ah, thanks for your help. We really appreciate it. Ah, we really do." With that, he left.

I went down to the hotel to find Rex Redux. People with suitcases bustled through the lobby. At the desk a skinny little clerk with pimples gave me the room number. The screenwriter and his personal photographer had a room on the third floor. The two of them sat in front of the television, watching news bulletins. Arnold Cohen sat at the desk typing away. He barely looked up.

"There he is!"

"We thought you'd skipped town." Rex Redux was glued to the TV. "This will go down as one of the great accidents of all time! This *is* going to go down like the wreck of the Hindenburg. Like the sinking of the Titanic. In the annals of technological accidents this is big!"

Arnold Cohen furiously typed away at the desk.

"My story made the front page of the California papers this morning," he beamed. "The Sunday edition! They say I can have the front page tomorrow if this story's as good. I'm just going to flood them with vivid reports."

He cracked his knuckles then furiously flailed away at the portable, occasionally stopping to pick up the phone and read his breathless copy over the line to some editor in California. He spouted over the phone, "One knowledgeable source was quoted as saying this was the biggest technological accident since the wreck of the Hindenburg."

Rex Redux handed me a crisp fifty dollar bill.

"We desperately need here some smoke and a six-pack of beer. You know the town, kid. We're counting on you."

The smoke was easy. A friend of mine uptown was still home. The beer was a different matter. Most all the barkeeps had evacuated. Finally I found an open bar just a few blocks from the hotel. I walked the deserted streets back to the hotel, the six-pack under my arm.

"We thought maybe you'd skipped to Mexico with the fifty," Rex Redux laughed.

Lance Cullpepper made a grab for the smoke. He sat in front of the TV rolling joint after joint, chain smoking. They were watching the local news. The local paper and TV stations soothingly reported the situation at the reactor was under control. I told Rex Redux that fear seemed to swing like a pendulum.

"It's been a pendulum of fear for the last few days. One moment you're scared shitless, then things calm down, then the fear swings back worse than before."

As I said this the network news came on. Rex Redux turned his attention to the tube, cutting me off. The network quoted unnamed sources as saying the reactor might blow sometime during the night. A brightly colored graphic depicting a violent reactor explosion lit our faces.

That was all Rex Redux had to see. It was like someone had lobbed an information grenade into the room. Jumping up, he paced madly about the room, pulling his hair. What in the name of God was he doing in a shit-ass little town like this! he yelled. Who had talked him into it? How could he die in a place like this? He had to get the hell out.

Lance Cullpepper, a joint in his mouth, his head enveloped in a cloud, confessed this was the most scared he'd ever been in his life.

"Vietnam was nothing like this."

Hysteria fed on itself.

"They're expecting a big explosion all right!" Rex Redux threw back. "Did you see the size of those damn concrete blast shields they were bringing in this morning? We might as well just kiss our asses good-bye."

"Knowledgeable sources say concrete blast shields have been shipped to the reactor site," Arnold Cohen sputtered over the phone.

Rex Redux took a pull of beer. He calmed down.

"It *is* a pendulum of fear," he sighed.

I told them I was heading for the mountains. Did they want to come along? Rex Redux was no longer frightened. Maybe he wouldn't die tonight, after all. He seemed exhausted, wrung out from the scare. He and Lance Cullpepper would be more comfortable in the hotel, he allowed, sinking back down into the bed.

I asked Arnold Cohen if he wanted to spend another night at the house. He shook his head no.

"I'm going to stay here with Rex and Lance," he said.

I could see he was mad at me, but I couldn't tell if it was because I'd given Chrisandra Young Sterling's bed last night or because I'd called him an asshole that afternoon. Wonder, wonder.

"Look, Cohen, I'm sorry I called you an asshole."

"Oh, forget it."

Months later Arnold Cohen and Rex Redux together would sign a book deal to write about the meltdown. For all I know the two of them had already cut a deal when they'd decided not to take me along on the interview with the red-haired technician.

I left the three of them in their cloud of smoke. While I walked down the hall I could still hear Arnold Cohen delivering his vivid reports over the phone.

29.

When I got back to the house it was dark. Sterling was waiting on the porch.
"Do you still want to go?"
She shook her head yes.
We took her truck. We drove through the dark deserted streets. I made her stop at my parents' house. The big stone house sat dark and forboding in the night.
"You never were inside my parents' house, were you?"
She shook her head no.
"Let me show you."
Inside all the paintings had been taken from the walls, the silver from the drawers. The folks had left in a hurry. The blank spots on the walls stared out at us. We sat down on the stairway, looking up at the grand staircase.
"This is where I grew up."
"Maybe we should go."
She took my hand, pulled me from the steps. We went back to the truck. Tony and Beth's cabin was all the way out by the Appalachian Trail. It was cold up in the hills. We drove up into the mountains not saying much. The cabin was damp and

sullen. First I tried lighting a fire in the stove but I couldn't get the flue open. The place filled with smoke. Coughing, I opened a window. Sterling sat down on the sofa. I sat down on the chair. The cabin was cluttered with junk. We moved toward each other, twisting our way through the junk between us on the floor, our bodies twisting at odd angles, arms reaching for each other, the things between us melting away. In each other's arms.

"Tom. Please. Let's go home."

"You're so hard, you know that? You're so very hard to please."

To love her was an exercise of trust, an act of danger, like the time I'd cut her hair. I knew then that someday I would have her. The universe might collapse and expand, time might come to an end and begin again, this world might turn to dust and be remade, but I would have her.

I let her go. We straightened our clothes. Half smiling, we stumbled out to her truck. A light drizzle had begun to fall. All the way back to town we didn't say a word. I watched the cold rain splash on the windows of the truck, feeling I'd lived this moment a million times before and would live it a million times more. She parked the truck in front of the house. We went inside.

"Please don't leave me alone tonight," I said to her.

We sat down in chairs on opposite sides of the living room. We slept like that till morning, in our heavy coats.

30.

In the morning I went to the office to read the papers. Someone somewhere had decided the crisis was over. The papers were all saying the hydrogen bubble in the reactor had mysteriously shrunk during the night. Lenny Popadopolis came in.

"Didn't we tell you?" he beamed. "The meltdown's over. Our psychic was right." He picked up the phone and called his psychic in Chicago.

"Let me talk to her."

He handed me the phone. The psychic was a sweet-sounding middle-aged woman. My curiosity got the best of me. I asked her what the future held for me. She asked for my name. She repeated it slowly, the words of my name rolling slowly off her tongue.

"Why, someday you'll be famous." She said this suddenly, sounding surprised herself. "And you'll have some joy and you'll have some sorrow."

"There's more good news," Lenny Popadopolis went on, hanging up the phone. "Because we predicted the meltdown they've invited us on That's Incredible."

"'Us?'"

"We mean, just ourselves."

I walked back to the house. Rex Redux and Lance Cullpepper sat with Sterling in the living room. The movie writer said he was glad to see me. His advance check had just come. He wanted me to take him to my bank so he could cash it, so he could eat lunch. We were getting ready to go when I got a call from a Washington Post reporter. He thanked me for helping their man last night.

"There'll be a by-line in it for you," he promised before hanging up.

I left the house with Rex Redux to cash his advance check. While we were going out the door Lance Cullpepper had Rex Redux and me pose together for a photo in the alley. It was shaping up to be a nice day. The sun was burning off the rain from last night. Rex Redux looked appreciatively down the alley at the row of century-old frame houses.

"I'd forgotten how nice it is here in the East," he said. "How nice all the old buildings are."

We climbed into Rex Redux's rented Lincoln. Just before we pulled off Sterling came running from the house yelling that the Philadelphia newspaper was on the phone.

"I'll call back."

"You certainly are doing well for yourself," Rex Redux said as we drove off. "Those reporters with the Post will remember you. You'll be able to work with them again in the future if something else comes up." He said he'd been talking to Sterling about me before I'd come in. "You'll have to remember, kid, all this attention is temporary. Fleeting. The national press is like a spotlight."

Saying this he dramatically lifted his hands from the wheel, popping them open, like a spotlight coming on. "It's very bright when it hits. But soon the beam will shine somewhere else. You should be ready for that. Some people are depressed when it happens." He lectured me about this and that. If ever I came to Hollywood he'd teach me how to write a movie. "I'll teach you everything I know. It'll only take five minutes." He laughed. "Hell, here it is in a nutshell: All movies have five elements in their formula. The introduction. Character development. Crisis. The chase scene. Conclusion."

I was so impressed I took out my pad and made notes. I still have the notebook with the hurriedly scrawled five-line essence of Hollywood. A few years later I finally saw his movie and laughed at an inane chase scene involving Jack Lemmon and a carload of nuclear industry thugs.

"By the way," he turned to me, "the magazine wants me to write seven thousand words." He seemed embarrassed about something.

"Yes?"

"How many typewritten pages is a thousand words?"

"Three and a half to four, double-spaced."

The only open branch of the bank was out at the shopping mall. Unfortunately for Rex Redux I'd emptied my account the previous Friday. The check was for seven hundred and fifty and I wouldn't have had enough money to cover it anyway. The teller got on a phone, checked my account, then came back, refusing to cash Rex's check.

"Look at the check!" Rex Redux told the teller loud enough for everyone waiting in line to hear. "It's from a nationally known magazine. Would they write a bad check?" The teller was an unimpressed middle-aged woman with graying hair. She said the bank's policy prevented her from cashing the check if he didn't have an account.

"What about him? He has an account."

"Mr. Parker has insufficient funds in his account."

Rex Redux demanded to speak to the branch manager. The assistant branch manager, a pudgy fellow in his early thirties, came out. Rex Redux loudly restated his case. The assistant bank manager listened, then calmly refused to cash the check. Rex Redux got louder. He demanded to speak to the manager, not his brickhead assistant. The manager was out of town, the assistant said. No, he wouldn't telephone him, the assistant said.

"All right, all right, are you ready for this?" Rex was yelling, no longer trying to suppress his tantrum. "Are you ready?"

"I'm ready."

"Do you know who I am?" Rex named the nuclear meltdown movie that had terrified my friend Tony. "Have you heard of that?"

"Yes," the assistant manager allowed.

"Well I wrote that movie."

For a moment the assistant branch manager looked at Rex Redux.

"*I don't care,*" he said at last.

I was embarrassed. People were looking over. I kind of shrugged apologetically.

Rex Redux stormed off, yelling it was this sort of mentality that was responsible for the meltdown in the first place. We drove back to the house. When we got there Sterling's friend Patty, star-struck, was ogling Lance Cullpepper. Lance was showing her the glossy movie industry broadside he'd been carting around all weekend. When Rex came in she almost swooned.

"What was it like to work with Jane Fonda?" Patty wanted to know.

"Oh Jane's a beautiful person. She really is."

Rex Redux told Lance Cullpepper they had to find a place to cash the check if they ever wanted to eat lunch. They started to go. Patty, realizing they were getting away, ran after Rex with a pencil to get his home phone number in California.

Within the hour Rex Redux returned, saying he'd managed to talk some banker on the West Coast into wiring a line of credit against which he'd cashed the advance check. He reached into his pocket and handed me a hundred and fifty dollars.

"Here, kid," he said, "I want you to have this."

I don't know why he gave it to me. I guess he thought he owed me something. I hope I haven't given you the wrong impression of Rex Redux. He was all right in my book.

They were on their way out of town. Before going they wanted to swing by the reactor for one last look-around. I rode along. Behind the observation center an entire city of mobile homes had been tossed together for the scientists. Someone somewhere had billed this gathering of scientists "the greatest minds on earth." There they all were, before our eyes, the greatest minds on earth, living in a trailer park. Lance Cullpepper disappeared to snap pictures. Rex Redux and I strolled past the mobile homes. Tensions had eased noticeably. The emergency seemed over. There was an early morning cheeriness to the place. Birds chirped, the sun was shining.

It was hard to believe we were so close to a damaged nuclear reactor. Looking at the nuclear plant you couldn't tell it was damaged. The funny thing about the whole incident, I remarked to Rex Redux as we walked along, was that, externally, the nuke never looked any different. The domed reactor containment building sat as cold and stony as the day it'd been built. You'd never know anything was wrong. To a large degree the meltdown had happened inside us. The accident and panic by in large had taken place in our minds. But, of course, that's the worst place for an accident to happen. We strolled along until we came to a bald scientist who poked his head from the window of his mobile home, taking in the day.

"Excuse me, Doc. You're one of the greatest minds on earth, aren't you?" I asked.

"Oh, yes. Can't you tell?"

He patted his bald head.

"Well we're interested in interviewing only one of the top

ten minds. No use talking to lesser minds if we can avoid it. You are in the top ten, aren't you?"

"Sorry. I'm just the seventeenth greatest mind on earth. The top ten just stepped out to lunch."

"Oh well. Too bad."

We strolled around for quite awhile before I had them drive me home. Rex and Lance came in for a minute to say good-bye to Sterling. As they were leaving, as an afterthought, Lance Cullpepper gave me the glossy movie industry broadside he'd been flashing around all weekend. He kind of handed it to me like he didn't know what else to do with it. "Here, why don't you keep this." It was as if he was trying to convince me that he and Rex were really *Hollywood*.

I still have the glossy movie industry broadside tucked away in a shoe box someplace. Every once in awhile, while searching for something else, I'll come across it. The black, glossy paper is creased from all the handling Lance Cullpepper gave it that weekend. I'll take it out and eye the first page with the slick movie company logo. I'll open it up to the company list. Far down the long column I'll see Rex Redux's and Lance Cullpepper's names. Invariably, I'll smile.

31.

The day went by with no word from the Washington Post. I called the Post reporter.

"The deal's off," he told me.

He offered no explanation. I couldn't figure it out. Later that evening at the office I ran into Jack Falstaff, just back from his evacuation. He seemed cagier than usual.

"Did you know before I came to town I tended bar in DC?" he asked out of the blue.

"Yes, I think you once mentioned that."

"Did I ever tell you that some of my best customers at the bar were Post reporters?"

"So?"

"Well this morning a friend of mine called from the Post. A reporter friend of mine. He said they were negotiating with you for a by-lined article. He asked my opinion of you."

"What did you tell them?"

"I told him I thought you were already in way over your head, what with editing the magazine and your other freelance commitments."

"So that explains it! You badmouthed me to the Washington Post!"

He started to laugh, backing out of the room.

"Damn you Falstaff!"

"You little fuck, Parker. You shouldn't have fired me as copy editor. Revenge is sweet, isn't it?" He ran off down the steps.

32.

As for me, I barricaded myself in the middle room upstairs with my typewriter. I was on deadline and the phone wouldn't quit ringing. Sterling took messages so I could write.

A few weeks later I was at the office when I looked out the window and saw Sterling coming down the street. A copy of a magazine flapped under her arm. She yelled up through the window, "So now you're famous." I ran downstairs and surveyed my article. It wasn't the cover story. We'd lost out to the Bee Gees. Sterling was reserved, standing against the wall with her arms crossed, watching me with amusement.

"Are you happy?" she asked.

"Why shouldn't I be?"

"You could do better."

I didn't see how. To celebrate I took Sterling and her dogs out for a drive in the country. We went to visit her friend Patty at her cottage in the woods. Patty had a hat rack with a hat collection in one corner of her kitchen. While we talked and drank wine Sterling tried on hats. She finally settled for a ridiculous hunter's cap and a wild pair of reflective sunglasses. She tucked her hair up under the hat and looked like a man from

Mars. She revelled in her strangeness, taking in her image in the mirror, walking wordlessly around the kitchen, making the dogs bark. We went out for a walk in the woods and she kept the glasses on. You'd look in the lenses and see your own reflection.

We had dinner at Patty's house. It turned out she had a date with my friend Jim Robbins. She nervously asked us along so Robbins wouldn't try anything. So the four of us went to see a movie, Woody Allen's Manhattan. In the lobby of the theater Sterling took my arm and walked with me down the aisle to a seat up front.

"I don't see how he gets off calling it Manhattan," Sterling said when it was over. "There wasn't a single black, Oriental or Spanish-speaking person in it."

"Do you think they really make love in movies?" I asked. "Or is it fake?"

"Are you joking? It's Hollywood. It's all fake."

We all went out for a drink. The bar was fashionably art deco, the bar itself made of brass with mirrors and planters hanging down all over. We sat drinking beer at the brass bar.

"Here's to love," I said, raising my glass. "Let's all have a laugh in the face of love."

"Now you're sounding like F. Scott Fitzgerald," Patty laughed.

Sterling made up her mind to organize a protest march against the reactor. The town's twelve original anti-nukes weren't doing any organizing. Within a week five hundred people had joined the anti-nuclear group, and the twelve original anti-nukes, liberal gadfly malcontents at heart, were unable to cope with this sudden success. New members quickly plotted to get rid of the old. A series of loud accusatory meetings was held, which came to be known as the Gang of Four trials. There was a power struggle. No one was organizing.

Sterling got it in her head to organize a protest march for women and children.

"Women and children are most victimized by radiation, you know," she explained.

She'd begun running in a thousand directions, calling all around, talking to everyone, trying to line up speakers and entertainers. Somehow, through Rex Redux I think, she'd managed to get Joan Baez's phone number. She called up Joan Baez and asked if she'd perform at her rally. Joan Baez was shocked. She wanted to know who had given out her number.

"You just can't call me up! I'm Joan Baez!"

Sterling laughed as she told me about it, leaning her head in her hands.

"Joan Baez says she's not into nuclear power at the moment. She says South America's where it's at."

There was a big national anti-nuclear rally one weekend down in DC. One night I suggested to Sterling that she could raise money for her women's and children's march by selling flowers at the national rally.

I volunteered to order the daisies. A few days later I came home from work to find a note on the door, written from Sterling to her friend Hank, the medical student from Philadelphia. "Hank, come on in and make yourself at home, kiddo. Sterling." I went charging from the house, not even stopping to go inside. I spent the night at the office, in the feminists' bed. The next day when I returned home Sterling told me Hank had been unable to get in. Godwit, the German shepherd, barked and growled, wouldn't let him in.

I bought the dog a steak.

That night there was an editorial board meeting. Max, the unemployed silo inspector, leaned over and said he'd heard I was helping Sterling with her women's and children's march.

He was decked out in one of his Hawaiian shirts. "I didn't know you had a cunt," he chuckled. I left the meeting in disgust. Later I found out the editorial board had discussed whether Sterling was a lesbian. They'd actually taken a vote. To my surprise, Roger Henley, the art director, said he spoke from experience when he said Sterling wasn't gay. He volunteered to the board that they'd made love. Still, a vote was cast and she was found a lesbian, nine to six.

A few days later I was at the cash register paying for my lunch at the corner drug store when I backed into, of all people, Karen, the young woman on the bus who'd stood me up at the museum's mastodon bones all those months ago.

"I came by the office looking for you," she said. "They sent me down here."

We took my car downtown to an Italian restaurant near the train station. An old waiter with twitching red eyes gave us menus. We shared an order of antipasto. She played with her vegetables, smoked a cigarette.

"I think I may drive down to West Virginia to bring my friend Mike home for spring break."

"Really? That would be fun. Can I come?"

In the morning I picked her up. Karen ran around the kitchen making egg salad sandwiches for the trip. It was a nice drive. Most of the way down she sat in the bright mountain sun reading aloud to me from her diary. Silly, whimsical girl memories of summers past. We got to Morgantown late in the afternoon but Mike was nowhere in sight.

We killed time walking through the hilly streets, stopping at little shops along the way. Karen bought a small card explaining foot massage. The card described how the act of massaging various parts of the foot benefited corresponding parts of the body. "See here? Rubbing under the big toe's good for the liver, while a touch of the arch can cure ulcers in the digestive tract." We wound down through the streets, into the student union building.

By the time we strolled back to the dorm Mike was in. Karen knocked around his little room. "I like this campus," she said. "Maybe it'd be nice to go to school here." With that she went off searching for the admissions office.

Mike gave me a quizzical look.

"Where's Sterling?"

I told him about finding the note to Hank on the door, about how the dog wouldn't let him in.

"You should buy that dog a steak."

"I did."

"I don't know what it is with you and Sterling. You can't be natural around each other. You're always tripping off each other's alarm signals." Then, after some thought, "Sterling really cares about you, you know. You should have heard her taking your messages on the phone while you were working."

He nodded at the door.

"What about her?"

I shrugged.

Karen returned. She had a few pamphlets from the admissions office. She asked if I'd walk with her outside. The two of us left the dorm and walked under some trees. She got out the egg salad sandwiches. As we walked along we ate. Suddenly she started crying. She wouldn't say why. She'd only say things had been easier when she'd been younger.

Mike came out with his things. He rode in the backseat. We didn't get home till late. We took Mike to his parents' place and followed him in to listen to records. After awhile Karen said she'd better get home herself.

We went out to my car. It was dark in the car and her face shone pale in the moonlight. Now she said she didn't want to go home. She was hungry. The only place open was Howard Johnson's. We ordered coffee and pie. Karen didn't eat a bite.

She sat across from me in the stall, not talking. I asked if she wanted to leave, but she only made eyes.

After I finally got her out of Howard Johnson's I drove her full speed to her house. She wouldn't get out of the car. I told her I was tired from all the driving and had to get some sleep. She wouldn't get out.

If somebody had a plan here it wasn't mine. I took her down to the office. We fell asleep together on the bed in the feminists' room. Nothing much happened. Groping, young attempts at lovemaking. I didn't want to keep her out all night but I fell asleep. When I opened my eyes the sun was up. Someone was downstairs in the anti-nukes office, running off copies on the mimeo machine. I knew it was Sterling, running off flyers for her protest march. It even sounded like Sterling, clanking around with the mimeo machine.

I woke Karen. She sat up, taking in the disheveled room.

"Where am I?" Slowly it came back to her. "Oh my God! It's morning! I've never been out all night before."

"What do you mean you've never been out all night before?"

"Just what I said. What will I tell my mother?"

I led her quietly down the steps and out the front door, the whole time listening to the sounds of the mimeo machine.

The next weekend Nate Freeman flew in from Seattle. He said he had a few days off so he'd hopped on a plane just for kicks. I couldn't shake the suspicion he wanted to check up on me and Sterling. The night of his arrival we had a big crowd over for dinner. Sterling was more nervous than usual as she rushed around getting ready. From the table I watched her comb her hair in the mirror above the kitchen sink. She wore a very pretty halter blouse.

"I don't know why I'm so nervous," she said. She sat down to a cup of tea at the table. She really looked beautiful. She hurriedly plopped the little tin tea ball around in the hot cup.

"Well yes I do. It's Nate. I think he's got this crazy idea of having some sort of serious relationship with me. I'm aware that the nature of relationships are continually changing but still it's so hard to know the right thing to do sometimes. The right thing to say."

"You're always intellectualizing. Try to feel for once and not worry about the right thing to say."

"And if you were in my position? What would you do?"

"If I were you I'd take up with me. That would put him off."

She wasn't helped by the advice.

Late in the afternoon people started showing up and I pulled beers from the refrigerator. Freeman made a grand entrance, with all the women hugging him and all. He came up and asked me how I was doing. I was a little stiff.

"I have a sudden back ache," I told him.

"What happened?"

"I don't know. It came on all of a sudden. Tension, I guess."

Freeman persuaded Patty to walk on my back. I got down on the carpet and she marched up my spine. It cracked loudly.

"A miracle! I'm good as new!"

"Sometimes that works."

Freeman told us about Jack Falstaff's recent triumphal trip to Seattle. Falstaff's luck had taken yet another fortuitous turn. Falstaff was hanging out in the anti-nukes' abandoned office one night shortly after the meltdown when he answered a telephone call from a woman working for an anti-nuclear group in Seattle. Opposed to a planned reactor, the group wanted to fly out an expert to testify at a hearing. They'd pay all travel expenses and foot the bill at a good hotel for a week. Would anyone be available?

They were in luck, Falstaff told her. He was available to testify.

They sent him a ticket and flew him out later in the week. Nate Freeman, working in Seattle, witnessed most of Falstaff's visit.

"It was a big town meeting," Freeman laughed, hardly believing it himself when he told the story. "Thousands of people turned out to debate the merits of nuclear energy in the Northwest. Someone stood up and told the city council, 'There's only one man here tonight who's truly qualified to talk on this issue.' The president of the city council asked who that might be, and would this distinguished person please come forward and give them the honor of hearing him speak. All eyes turned to the back in respectful silence as Jack Falstaff came tripping down the aisle. He really let them have it."

Nuclear reactors in the process of melting were so fearful a thing, he told them, he'd been forced to realize discretion was indeed the better part of valor and had repaired to the country. He was a great hit in Seattle. Freeman later went to see him at his hotel. He'd witnessed Falstaff pick up a fat woman in the hotel bar. The woman had been at the town hall performance and doted over Falstaff. Freeman came by Falstaff's room the next day and found Falstaff and the woman in bed. "Lying," Freeman said, "like beached whales under the sheets."

After dinner Freeman wanted to go down to the Open Hearth to listen to jazz. Sterling didn't want to go. She said she was tired and might try sleeping. Nothing we could say could convince her to come. We had a nice walk down to the bar. Inside the jazz was blowing. I ordered beer after beer and yelled over the music to Freeman.

"I think I'm in love with Sterling," I yelled to him.

"What?"

"I said I think I'm in love with Sterling."

He heard me, he said, he just couldn't believe his ears. He seemed a little off balance.

"You don't know what you're saying," he yelled back. "It's all this tension you've been under lately. The meltdown and everything. It was proven in World War II. In hideous Nazi death camp experiments people who thought they were about to die had a sudden subconscious urge to procreate. This is proven scientific fact I'm telling you. It's the life force trying to keep them alive." He was red-faced screaming this nonsense over the noise of the band.

"Are you equating my life with a Nazi death camp experiment?"

"If the shoe fits."

Sterling came in. She walked through the crowded bar, stopping to look around. She always stood out, even in a crowd, as if a light shone around her. I called her over. She said she couldn't sleep and had decided to join us after all. We stood side by side, merrily drinking beers.

"Do you two think you'll ever get together?" Freeman finally said. We stood there smiling and shrugging shoulders. He walked off into the crowd.

Early the next morning three hundred daisies were delivered to my door. It turned out not to be such a hot idea. We only sold enough daisies at the rally in DC to make our money back, maybe a little more. We had at least a hundred daisies left over. I brought the hundred leftover daisies back home and arranged them in buckets on the kitchen table.

That night the local anti-nukes threw a fundraiser in an old mansion along the river. By the time I got there the party was in full swing. Jenkins was there.

"One of the younger Kennedys just stopped by," he said, a drink in his hand. "Campaigning for his Uncle Ted. When he came in the women went wild. You should have seen it. Those Kennedys have something in their genes."

"They've a ton of money is what they have."

It was twilight. From the porch where Jenkins and I talked I suddenly saw Sterling walking down along the river, her silhouette outlined by the lights on the other side.

"Excuse me, Jenkins."

I went outside, down to the river, found her looking at the current.

"There you are," she said. "I wanted to talk."

We walked a little ways down the shore.

She turned to me.

"Tom. Can't we just be friends?"

"I'm afraid I don't like your taste in friends."

The next night I stopped in at the Open Hearth for a beer. Mike came in.

"I thought I'd find you here," he said. He ordered a draft. "Sterling called me," he said. He hadn't even taken a sip from his beer.

"She did? How'd she get your number?"

"Search me."

"What'd she want?"

"She wants me to have a drink with her at the hotel tomorrow night."

"You're not going, are you?"

"Why not? You can come along."

The next night I rode downtown with Mike. We got as far as the revolving door at the hotel. I couldn't bring myself to go in. Mike looked at his watch.

"Come on, Tom. Don't be that way."

"You go on. I'll catch up later."

I ran off down the dark street, looking at the hulking mass of the hotel over my shoulder. Already it was dark. I cut down to the river. A cool breeze came off the water. You could hear the water slowly going by. I walked as fast as I could up the bank, shadows from the weak moonlight splashing on my face, until I reached the office. I went up the steps and slept.

The next night I ran into Mike at a party. We were both trashed. As the party wore on Mike kept staggering around the

beer keg, filling his plastic cup, talking to friends.
"I was invited to go to Boston," he suddenly said.
I looked at him.
"I guess Tom doesn't want to hear about Boston," he said.
I walked away, but a little later I cornered him.
"Mike. I know back in school we used to like the same women. But let's make a pact. Stay away from Sterling, okay?"
"A pact? Why? She's the one who's been calling me."
"I wonder why."
"Tom. You just have to face it. She doesn't like you that way. She's not attracted to you that way. She told me herself. Last night. She just wants you as a friend."
"That's how I want you, Mike."

33.

Everything was collapsing and I had to get out. The next night, at midnight, Nate Freeman called.

"You want to drive to Maine for lunch? My sister's having a graduation party. We'll make it if we leave in half an hour."

I wasn't so sure about taking my car. It was still leaking antifreeze. I'd been dumping metal anti-leak pellets into the radiator, hauling water in the trunk. Well, lackaday, there's always the road.

Sterling baked a dozen blueberry and bran muffins and gave them to Freeman for the trip. We left a little after one in the morning, taking my car. I drove like a madman, straight up 81. Before we knew it we were in New York. We stopped at a little diner near the border, filled with faded men in weary coats. Above the counter hung a clock with revolving advertising signs. I sat drinking coffee, watching the different signs flip beneath the clock.

We went back out to my car and drove madly north. A little before dawn we almost wrecked into a herd of deer. I'd just come over a rise when I saw the deer through the mist. I'd just enough time to slam on the brakes.

"Jesus!"

"Wow. That was close!"

We'd come to a complete stop on the highway. We sat watching the deer stroll around us. They took their time about it. Finally I slowly drove through them.

Before long the sun came out, baking off the mist. When we got hungry we'd take out the bag of muffins Sterling had baked.

"You're not jealous of me?" I asked Freeman.

"Jealous? Why should I be jealous?"

They were a little part of her and I slowly ate each one.

By mid-morning we got to the ocean.

"We take this road the rest of the way up," Freeman said.

Sailboats and fishing boats crawled off shore. Floats from lobster traps dotted the water.

"Let's stop somewhere and stretch our legs."

We stopped at a pretty town with a bay. Near the road a cemetery cut up over a hill. In the cemetery we stopped at a stone commemorating a seventeenth-century woman who'd been unjustly accused by one of the town fathers of being a witch. A plaque told all about it. She'd been burned at the stake and buried in the cemetery. Shortly thereafter the granite in her tombstone mysteriously darkened, all except for the pattern of a cross, which you could still plainly see. This strange development had moved her accuser to recant his story. Then he'd killed himself.

"Kind of gives you the creeps, doesn't it?"

"I'll say."

We took the ocean route through Maine. The road ran horseshoes through countless rocky inlets and bays. The water beyond was steel blue and choppy, here and there throwing up little silver waves, little white trawlers and little colored buoys. The whole trip the car leaked watered-down antifreeze. Every few hundred miles I'd stop to throw in more water and anti-leak pellets. The coolant in my radiator looked like molten metal.

"Forget about it and just floor it into town," Freeman called from the car at our last water-fill stop, a few miles away.

"Easy for you to say. It's not your car."

"Oh come on. Just get in and drive. It's only a few more miles."

He was anxious to get to the party.

"The temperature gauge is already on red. I'm afraid of a fire."

At last we set off. The road ran down through town. We went straight to the party. A catered lawn party, overlooking a bay. The moment we arrived Freeman spotted a young woman, threw his arms around her and ran off. I didn't see him until later that night. I hung around town and felt lost. It was a graduation party and everyone was caught up in their own busy plans.

That night I drove out to a pond house in the woods where the students had their graduation dance. The pond house was beautifully made. Birch bark walls and tall ceilings. There was a great outdoor dance floor and a telescope off to the side in the woods where you could look out over the lake and study the sky. Later that summer the pond house caught fire and burned to the ground.

I finally caught up with Freeman. He was running around the pond house with another woman and barely had time for a word. After the dance broke up the place emptied out fast. Looking around I realized I was alone. I had to drive back to town over strange mountain roads, nearly getting lost. I crashed out on a sofa in his sister's house.

Maine turned out not to be the answer. The bare brown mountains, the deep blue ocean, and the clean air were lost on me. I couldn't wait to leave. Freeman had a return trip ticket to Seattle and later the next afternoon we left for Boston. We didn't have much to say the whole trip down. We got stuck in traffic outside Boston and he missed his plane by five minutes. We stood outside the airport, scratching our heads, not saying much. The stars were out and planes were flying low overhead.

"Great. The next plane out," Freeman said, "leaves from Kennedy Airport at seven in the morning. I have a friend in Connecticut where I think we can spend the night." He had a great address book, with friends just about everywhere.

We got back on the dark highway. Outside Hartford he called his friend. Surprised to hear from Freeman, she asked us over. She turned out to be a friendly, heavyset woman named Buhulia Shivers. She had a great shaggy dog. I don't know what kind of animal it was but it had pencil-thick curls of hair. It had just given birth to pups and milk dripped down the curls, all over the floor. Buhulia Shivers followed it around with a roll of paper towels, wiping up the milk, all the while chatting over old times with Freeman. Freeman just wanted to make small talk with Buhulia Shivers all night. I wasn't a very good guest.

"If I'm going to deal with Long Island traffic in the morning I better rest."

Chatting happily away, Buhulia Shivers led me down to her basement, where I encountered the biggest dollhouse I'd ever seen. It took up the whole basement. It was really a dollmansion, with floor after floor of miniature rooms, each filled with little stuffed bears. "I'm a collector of stuffed bears," Buhulia Shivers laughed. She gave me a sofa by the bear mansion, then turned off the light, but I felt hundreds of little stuffed-bear eyes staring at me.

I hardly got any rest. The whole night I could hear Freeman talking over old times with her. I don't know, maybe he was a bear in her collection. Between their talk and all those bears staring down at me I hardly caught a wink. At five thirty Freeman came down and told me we had to be going. I was dead tired.

Already the freeways into New York were filling up. I drove like a mad automaton, like everyone else. We made Kennedy just in time. I walked Freeman to the ticket counter.

"Well it's been fun," he said.

We shook hands.

"Yeah it's been a blast."

By the time I got home I was nearly dead of exhaustion. When I parked the car it kind of coughed, then sputtered and went dead. The metal pellets I'd added to the coolant fused the engine. I never was able to start it again.

I bummed around town for a few days, not wanting to go back to the house. I holed up on the third floor of the office, in the feminists' room. There I was, living in dissipation in one of the rooms at the office, like Falstaff had been doing when I met him.

Sterling saw my car one night and tried to come over for a visit. I heard knocking on the door, looked out the window and saw her truck, but I wouldn't let her in. In the morning I found a note on my windshield. "Why do I get a feeling you're trying to avoid me?"

Later that day she called.

"What is it that you want from me?" she asked over the phone.

I said nothing.

"Please try to understand," she said. "I don't want to have any more relationships with men."

"What about Hank?"

"I promised myself if things didn't work out with Hank I'd never see another man. And right now things aren't going so well."

I didn't know what to say. She made me promise to stop by and see her.

The next night I came by the house. We went out to a sub

shop. The beer and sandwiches came and both of us started crying. I don't know what our waitress thought, seeing Sterling and me sitting at the table crying in our beer and all. After we ate we went out driving. It was a nice night. We drove across the river, then stopped at a store for popsicles. We each bought one. We drove to a park overlooking the river and the city, walked down through the dark lawn. Climbing up on a jungle gym, eating our popsicles, we looked into the night. The skyline of the city blinked in the background, the lights all moving and shimmering in reflections on the dark river.

When we got tired of staring into the night I took her home. I walked with her down the alley.

"Want to come in?"

I shook my head no.

We threw our arms around each other, holding on for the longest time. Stars were shining above our heads.

I came for my things the next day. She left a note saying she'd found me just when she'd needed me most.

A few nights later I was reading in the office when I heard light footsteps coming up the stairs. Too light for Falstaff. Too halting for Sterling. The footsteps got to the top of the stairs then made the turn down the hall. From out of the darkness emerged the face of Kate, Mike's friend from school. She was wearing a pretty beach dress. She came into the room and stepped in front of me, smiling.

"Well Kate. What a surprise. What brings you here?"

"Would you believe *you?*"

"I'm speechless."

"I wanted to tell you how much I enjoyed your recipes."

"Recipes? What recipes?"

"For the bread and ice cream. I borrowed my grandma's ice cream freezer and made the best strawberry ice cream."

"You didn't come all the way from West Virginia to tell me

that."

"No."

She was looking around the cluttered office. She had a big beach hat that she held behind her back.

"I don't believe I've ever seen a more cluttered bulletin board. Why doesn't someone clean it off?"

She started to remove a thumbtack.

"Don't! It's bad luck!"

"Bad luck? How do you mean?"

"Take my word. That bulletin board and I got through a nuclear meltdown and a broken romance. God knows what might've happened if I'd cleaned it off."

She laughed, tilting her head.

"Where's Mike?" I asked.

"I don't know. He told me he didn't want to see me anymore. He said he was confused."

"There's a lot of that going around."

"I was on my way to the shore. I stopped at your house. Sterling said you'd probably be over here. I wanted to see if you'd like to go to the beach with me."

I looked at her. Her hair was braided on either side of her head.

"Why the hell not?"

We took off a few minutes later, as soon as I could throw a few things into my sack. She had a little red car. We took turns driving, talking excitedly about whatever came into our heads. The whole way we blasted the radio. We kept heading east till we hit the ocean. We had no idea where we were. At first we could only smell the water but we came over a rise and there was a deep swatch of blue ahead. A desolate strip of beach stretched before us. We left the car at the road and ran down the dunes to the ocean. Kate took off her sandals and walked along the water's edge. I did the same. In the distance we could see a little town.

We walked along the edge of the water, carrying our shoes in our hands, until we hit the town. The town was set in an inlet and boats were going in and out. You could see the flash of sails almost all the way to the horizon. It was a small fishing village. We came up from the water and walked along the docks. It was a hot day and the air felt close. Somewhere, about the time we were walking up from the docks, Kate knit her arm around mine. We were both hot and sweaty and bumping around as we walked and her arm wrapping around mine was almost an incidental thing, a hot swirl of air wrapping around another hot swirl of air, our breath lingering around us as we came up the sand into the little town, the sea lapping at the shore behind us the whole time.

The town was mostly a one-street affair. A pack of dogs rambled down one of the side streets. A young boy on a bicycle with training wheels spun in circles on the lazy main drag. We came off the street at a big old seafarers' saloon. We sat at the bar and ordered beers, which came in great icy steins. There was a special on clams and we each had a dozen. While we sat eating, a little girl came in with a jug for beer for her father. She spun around clutching the filled jug, ran out the door. The bartender came over with two small paper cups and placed them in front of us. "The fella down there bought you two a round." We looked down the bar to an old salt who smiled toothlessly, gave us a bob of his head.

By the time we got out of the bar the sun was red and going down. We walked past the quiet docks, the fishing boats all in and tied down for the night. Pleasure boats hung closer to shore, bobbing in the gentle swells. Some quality of sand at the edge of an ocean, as the foam settles in and the sand settles down, makes it seem like the only real and solid thing in the world. We walked along the edge of the water.

"Why did you and Mike break off?"

"Let's not talk about it. Why talk about anything?"

We walked along the edge of the water watching the sunset. The streets shrunk into a lit-up memory behind us. Somewhere on the other side of the town a lit-up Ferris wheel spun slowly in the night. We came to a high set of dunes. We walked over and sat down in the cool sand.

"I love this temperature," Kate said, running her hands along her arms. "You can't feel the air. You can't feel your skin. It's neither hot nor cold."

Now it was night.

"I could use a swim," she said. Stripping off her clothes she ran down into the surf.

"Oh, Tom the water's wonderful. Aren't you coming in?"

I followed her in. We played and laughed. When she got tired of the water she walked up the beach and fell into the sand. I followed her out and fell beside her and we kissed.

A few days later, after I got back to town, I was sitting in the hotel listening to jazz when Mike came in. He came up to the table and stood staring down at me.

"Well Mike. You're back from Boston."

"Boston? I wasn't in Boston."

"Well what a shame. We all thought you were in Boston."

He stood there staring down at me.

"Well should I bust you on the nose? Isn't that what I'm supposed to do?"

"What are you talking about?"

"You know damn well what I'm talking about. Kate."

"She told you?"

"I made her tell. Now I want you to tell me the rest of it. Every last detail."

"Like hell. I was the one who wanted to have a pact. But you wouldn't have it, remember? You were the one who broke it off with Kate so you could go off to Boston, isn't that it? 'She's not attracted to you that way,' you told me."

"You're crazy."

"What about Sterling?"

"I can't figure her out. She's too complicated for me."

"Welcome to the club."

He stood there sort of fuming, his shoulders hunched.

"Ah, we can't let these women come between us, Mike. How about a beer?"

He sat down.

"Women."

"Yeah. Women."

We took turns ordering rounds.

"We've got to keep things in perspective, Mike. No use letting things get to us."

"Yeah, there's no use in that."

I only saw Sterling North one or two times after that. My car conked out, once again I rode the bus uptown. It was rush hour, and the bus was crowded. Sterling got on and stood in the aisle across from me. She didn't even see me until I stood to get off the bus. I reached my hand up and pulled the cord. Then I got off the bus.

A few weeks later I wrote to her apologizing for the way I'd acted, but heard nothing back. I wrote several letters but heard nothing back.

Several months went by. I was out driving downtown one day in my father's car when I saw her walking down by the river. I honked the horn and waved for her to get in. She did. She wasn't too talkative. I offered to drive her to her door but she panicked. She had me drop her a block away.

"Have a good journey," she said, closing the door. I watched her walk away.

A few weeks later Nate Freeman went to see her and told me she was living with a guy she'd known since high school. She was running around doing his laundry and washing his dishes.

I always had trouble figuring her out. It was as if she'd retreated to a safer, easier time in her life. She moved out West with the guy and hasn't been heard from since.

Nate Freeman soon tired of corporate life and quit his job in Seattle. He'd saved up enough money to buy the van. He fell in love with a beautiful young woman and together they took off in the van, traveling all around North America. One day he pulled up in his van and introduced me to his new friend, insisting the three of us drive to Gettysburg to see the battlefield.

"I don't know why I took that job," he told me as we strolled past the monuments to the fallen soldiers. "Life's too short not to do what you want."

"I couldn't agree more." I no longer cared so much about my own Godalmighty career. Some era in both our lives was ending, I knew.

One day not long after that I was rooting through my things when I came across a box of waxed lips and a popsicle stick. Emerson said all we're really looking for in life is someone to tell us to do our best. I guess that's what Sterling North was for me.

Years passed. I was sitting in a restaurant late one afternoon when I heard two diners talking excitedly about a reactor that had just blown up somewhere in Russia. I hope you weren't expecting me to tell you there's another, better life somewhere just up ahead, blinking in the distance like lights across the water and all that Fitzgerald crap.

Not long ago I went alone into the woods and found myself hiking back through the winding paths to the remains of the cabin called Paradise where I'd once taken Sterling. It was little more than broken boards and rubble. The first time I'd seen the place I was sixteen years old, working as a counselor at a summer camp for retarded kids on the other side of the mountain. One weekend an adventurous friend of mine, also working at the camp as a counselor, took off alone up into the mountains. When he returned he spoke of a beautiful cabin in the woods. It was named Paradise. It was made of hand-hewn logs with a stone masonry fireplace and stone paths leading out of the woods. There was a bed and a summer kitchen, with utensils for weary journeyers to use. A sign asked only that it not be destroyed.

The next weekend we took fifteen or twenty retarded kids up the mountain. We stayed at a campsite near the cabin called Paradise. One of the other counselors took a troublemaking kid to the cabin and locked him inside, saying it was a jail. The kid went nuts, trashing the cabin, breaking windows and knocking down the masonry fireplace. The counselor joined in, distressed that the place looked so nice. By the time we got there it was over.

Years later I stood in the woods holding the decaying broken sign that read Paradise, thinking about Sterling, thinking about the days of my youth when I'd run so carefree through the woods.

WILLIAM KEISLING is a widely published writer of fiction, nonfiction and essays. His fiction has appeared in The North American Review, Rolling Stone, The Crescent Review, The New Southern Literary Messenger, Detroit News' Michigan magazine and Chicago's Aim magazine, among others. He's the author of four books. He lives with his small family in Pennsylvania.